GW00722724

About the Author

David Burt was evacuated from London to Yorkshire at the outbreak of the 2nd WW and his education suffered accordingly. He started work on a building site at fifteen and a half and had a variety of job roles before becoming the CEO of a UK manufacturing company making components for Aerospace, and electrical connectors for Formula 1 Race cars. During his career he was County Chairman for the CBI and on the Advisory Council for the BBC, before becoming the Chairman of the Regulatory Council for UK Optical services, he remains Chairman of the Consumer Complaints Service. He is a lifelong sculptor and has exhibited at the RA Summer Exhibition, he also rallies Classic Cars.

To my 10 Grandchildren

David Burt

SHORT SURPRISES

A CIP catalogue record for this title is available from the
British Library.

ISBN 9781785548208 (Paperback)
ISBN 9781785548215 (Hardback)

www.austinmacauley.com

First Published (2015)
Austin Macauley Publishers Ltd.
25 Canada Square
Canary Wharf
London
E14 5LQ

Printed and bound in Great Britain

Acknowledgments

To my daughter Sally-Anne for getting me started and my PA, Janet Hodge, for support with typing this manuscript.

Contents

A BOYHOOD PROJECT

Harold looked out of his bedroom window as he put on his dressing gown, looking from his vantage point up Clovelly Avenue, pleased as he always was that his house at the end of the row was the only one with a garage tacked on to the side. The garage that he and Muriel had always felt made them a cut above the other householders in the neat little row of houses.

Harold continued to stare up the Avenue with the returned sense of loss that Muriel was no longer with him. His senses were suddenly flooded with memories from their last peaceful days together in the hospice, where the staff had been so marvellous in making Muriel's passing so peaceful and calm.

Harold squared his shoulders, determined to concentrate upon the future by reminding himself it was his birthday in a week and he had a plan for the day, and he was going to see the first step of his plan put in place today. He had his customary breakfast of fruit and fibre cereal, sitting at the yellow topped table in the tidy kitchen.

The kitchen had been Muriel's pride and joy and in the few days since the funeral Harold had made sure the kitchen was impeccably tidy, every spoon, fork, cup and bowl in its customary place, just as Muriel would want it.

Thoughts of the funeral brought back the disconcerting thoughts that not having any children, and as far as he knew neither he nor Muriel having surviving family, the next stage of his life Harold reminded himself, without Muriel, would inevitably be rather lonely.

All these thoughts crowded in on him as he reconsidered the dramatic change he had committed himself to face a couple of hours from now.

To steady his nerves Harold took out a writing pad from the top drawer of the china cupboard, moving aside the memo board that Muriel had always used to methodically list her items to be purchased before they both visited the supermarket each week, and he then wrote the words 'Birthday List' on the top of the page.

Harold smiled sadly to himself, knowing there would not be a birthday 'day out' as there had always been with Muriel. His thoughts went back to the grand day they had visiting the Classic Car Show on his birthday of last year and, sighing, he concentrated on the list and wrote 'Sell the Honda'. He did not feel he was letting Muriel down as she liked the neat little silver car that was easy to park but he was sure she would be supporting his idea.

Harold reconsidered his 'Birthday List' that had been triggered by the unexpected phone call yesterday from the Maintenance Manager at the garage where he had worked. Coming out of the blue, Harold ran through the call in his mind.

"Hi, Harold, look just a call which Mr Farnworth thought you might be interested in. You know that project you were always going to take on 'one day'? Well, the opportunity has turned up today. Could you come down to the works?"

Harold went back to concentrating on his list, thought for a minute, and then wrote 'The miles I need to drive each year'. He struggled a bit as he listed the bank, supermarket, library, and garden centre and after some further thought 'days out' – say 4,000 miles. He then noted 'Money' and sucked his pencil as he thought about the amount of money he might need to find but stiffened his resolve by reminding himself he had his Post Office savings account and the holiday money fund. "After all," he thought, "I'm not likely to go off to Bournemouth for two weeks as Muriel and I had planned in the summer."

Harold finished his breakfast and fed the budgerigar, clicking his tongue to encourage the bird's chirping as he did so, reminding himself he would need to change the sandpaper liner in the cage the very next morning. Then, telling the budgerigar, "If I don't do the project now I never will", Harold felt sure the bird's happy chirping indicated her full support for his project.

Thus decided, Harold went upstairs and changed into a clean blue shirt and put on his old RAF tie, the tie he always wore on formal occasions. Carefully sliding his slacks off their hanger, putting them on and then making sure his dark blue silk handkerchief was in his blazer top pocket, he carefully studied his appearance in the long mirror just outside the bathroom, thinking Muriel would probably have found something to criticise, possibly the standard of polish on his shoes or the crease in his slacks.

None the less Harold felt satisfied with his appearance and let himself out of his front door and nodded to his inquisitive neighbour, Mrs Hilda Barnthorpe, who was as ever sitting in her front room watching every move in the Avenue. As far as Harold could tell, she watched all day observing each resident or visitor, tradesperson, service technician, or anybody who ventured into her field of focus.

Harold had never actually spoken to Mrs Hilda Barnthorpe. Their entire dialogue over several years had been conducted by him waving his right hand, occasionally in a sweeping motion when the weather was right or he was feeling in a good mood. Otherwise a rather stiff raise of the hand sufficed for the normal neighbourly politeness. Mrs Hilda Barnthorpe's only acknowledgement to Harold's communications was to nod her head forward, exposing her grey bun.

Making his way towards his garage door for his ten o'clock appointment this morning, Harold was sufficiently motivated by events to give Mrs Hilda Barnthorpe a sweeping hand salute of some forty-five degrees and he was encouraged to note she gave him something of a surprised nod of the head. As he opened the garage door he realised he was not entirely sure how he had discerned 'surprise' but he felt sure he had.

Driving the Honda along the road towards his old workplace was, Harold decided, a slightly surreal experience. He had spent so many years getting to the garage workshop for eight every morning that he knew every corner, curve and traffic island and all the points of hold up, but somehow driving now for his ten o'clock appointment the journey seemed entirely different.

Harold recalled the events of his leaving as he drove towards his appointment. It was only, he thought, about fifteen months ago he had finally 'retired' as he remembered Mr Farnworth saying, "Not because the company had the slightest concern over Harold's engineering skills or expertise, and they would miss his experience, but Head Office are worried because of his age and Health and Safety matters."

Mr Farnworth had not elaborated what the Health and Safety 'matters' might be but his tone had suggested the matter had been taken out of his hands and been decreed by a higher being!

Driving past the Post Office, Harold recalled he had felt as if life as he knew it had been suddenly and unexpectedly terminated, and despite the 'Retirement Dinner' and much 'good willing' from his colleagues, thought Harold as he drove along the High Street, the enjoyment of his days in the motor and mechanical world abruptly finished, and with it much of the excitement in his life.

Harold turned into the forecourt of the premises of LME Motor Services, noting as he did so that the direction signs indicating the way to the Service Reception, Sales

Office, etc. had not been washed clean by the apprentice. Otherwise, Harold thought as he parked the Honda in front of the showroom window, the place looked clean and the show area was filled with highly polished, modern motor cars.

Gladys, the receptionist, came round the desk to give Harold a hug. "How lovely to see you," she cooed. "Hope you are going to be happy with your project." She said this conspiratorially, edging close to Harold. "I can tell you EVERYONE, even Mr Farnworth, hopes you will agree so I hope they can sort out a deal. Mr Black, you know, young Giles is going to see you. He has just been made up to Sales Manager. I can't believe it, it wasn't ten minutes ago he was bringing the tea round." She laughed at the thought.

Almost exactly on queue young Giles shot out of the sales manager's office, hand outstretched so far that his double back shirt cuff and rather elaborate gold-plated car cuff links clearly demonstrated his new managerial status. He crossed the sales room floor at some speed, smile at the ready, giving Harold the fleeting impression he was going to be run over.

Giles gripped Harold's hand firmly in both of his and, Harold thought following Gladys' comments, it's hard to believe that only two years ago the embrace would have covered him in shop floor lubricating grease!

Giles' progress and enthusiasm was honest enough, Harold thought, as Giles looked briskly inside, outside and under the bonnet of the Honda. "Super," he said, "I'll have no bother at all finding a home for this little lady. Just what I would have expected with any car you own. Let's go and talk over the project details over a cup of tea."

Tea and biscuits followed as Giles repeated what Harold already knew from the previous day's telephone conversation. The 1934 Morgan two-seater Plus 4 with a Coventry Climax four cylinder engine ports had been taken in to sell as a favour by a relation of the owner of LME Motor Services, as the 90 year old owner of the Morgan, who had owned the Plus 4 for forty years, was no longer able to drive but was most anxious that the sports car went to someone who would know how to look after it.

LME Motors did not handle classic cars or sports cars but when the Managing Director had discussed his family commitment with Mr Farnworth, he recalled he had often discussed with Harold the boyhood dream Harold had of owning a Morgan, just as his father had. Mr Farnworth had been able to assure the Managing Director that nobody could be better suited to look after the old Morgan than Harold, providing an exchange deal could be struck, and the Managing Director, much relieved, had said, "Just do it at the best price you can."

The two-seater Morgan, with hood down, stood rather independently in the centre of the otherwise empty service bay.

Giles turned on the fluorescent lights and suddenly the dark blue marvel of the old two-seater stood out with its black cast wheels, its large chrome separate headlights with a central spotlight between reflecting and sparkling in the fluorescent lights. Harold noted the fold flat windscreen, the two chrome petrol filter caps behind the seats and he nodded as he walked around the Morgan. Looking at the two hill climb spare tyres he felt the beautifully patinated blue leather seat backs, and ran his hand over the faded polish of the wooden dashboard, noting with pleasure the Smith's instruments for engine revolutions and car speed, the oil, petrol gauges, all in harmony, Harold thought, with the magnificent 1930's design of a true, blueblood, British sports car.

Harold's reverie was abruptly brought back to the service bay by Giles' cough. "Sorry to have to mention it, Harold," said Giles, "but the best I can do is to take the Honda in for £3,500 and Mr Farnworth says I have to ask you how much you can afford for the Morgan." He coughed again anxiously. "This is a special project. I mean could you make a contribution of, say, £5,000 plus the Honda?"

Giles started a carefully rehearsed speech about a hire purchase arrangement before Harold cut him short with, "I will give you a cheque today."

At 4.14 p.m. the following Wednesday afternoon, Harold had his garage door open and was standing in his overalls, with his grease gun in his hand, having just completed one out of the long list of maintenance checks he was happily giving the Morgan when he became aware that a group of three schoolboys, in their St James' School blazers, standing on the pavement staring at the Morgan.

The tallest 16 year old said, "Afternoon Mr Pilgrim, what's the new motor you got?" Harold recognised the boy as a resident of Clovelly Avenue, without recalling a name. A second boy chipped in, "It's old ain't it?" Harold explained to them it was a Morgan: English designed and English built.

The more talkative leader pronounced again, "Oh right, that motor has got a wooden body then, has it?"

Harold tried to explain to the three lads that, "Whilst the framework is wooden, with aluminium panels, the chassis is steel."

The boys' interests were clearly not with the technical details and the rather one sided conversation deteriorated into, "My Dad's VW would see that 'old lady' off any day and bet you get drowned when it rains. Does it carry a bilge pump?" More laughter from the two who then drifted off up Clovelly Avenue, leaving the one quiet boy who then said, "Sorry, Mr Pilgrim," in a shamefaced way before he too wandered on his way up the road.

Harold took no concern at the boys' comments, far too agreeably immersed in his fortune at being able to realise a lifetime's dream, and one he reminded himself for the umpteenth time, for a cost that he would have doubled, perhaps tripled, even though this would have taken every spare pound he had. His thoughts were disturbed by the quiet young man, who had returned now in casual clothes, standing by the gate post.

"Hi, Mr Pilgrim. My mum says I should come and apologise for making such derog ... derogatory ... remarks earlier." Harold smiled. "You did not make derogatory remarks. What is your name?"

"Fred," said Frederick.

"Would you like to take a look at the Morgan?" asked Harold.

Later that very afternoon Harold had driven the Morgan to get his modest shop from the supermarket and having 'communicated' as usual with Mrs Hilda Barnthorpe, was opening his front door whilst juggling his grocery bags, when he heard his name called. He turned to be told by the pleasant looking lady standing on the pavement, that she was Fred's mother. Harold was immediately anxious. "I do hope you did not mind me keeping Fred for half an hour. He seemed so interested in my old car."

"He loved the visit," the lady replied. "I'm here to see you about another matter. I live at No. 20 up the road and I work in the hospice that looked after your wife in her last few days. Oh, I am sorry I should have introduced myself. I'm Joan Blake. Your wife Muriel and I got along really well and she told me how worried she was that you would be lonely on your own, and she was particularly worried about you being on your own this Saturday for your birthday. So I promised her, and she was very pleased and relieved, that I would invite you to tea with my husband Bill, and Fred and me – will you come?"

Harold put his parcels down and went across to the gate. "That really is nice of you, Mrs Blake. I would be delighted to come to tea on Saturday. Why this has really cheered me up. I'm so glad you got along with Muriel as I'm sure your friendship will have helped her enormously."

Saturday's tea party was a great success with a lovely home baked fruit cake and a single candle, that Harold had to blow out twice so that Fred could catch the image properly on his mobile phone.

Joan also provided a surprise by producing a leaflet from the hospice which was both information about an upcoming Classic Car One Day Rally to help raise funds, and an entry form. Both she and Bill wondered if Harold would take the Morgan with Fred as navigator to help raise the money that the hospice needed to keep their door open

Fred had clearly been told by his parents not to ask Harold to take him on the rally but his suppressed excitement as he sat round the tea table was quite enough for Harold to enquire if he would interested? Would he just!

The event went brilliantly. No. 65, Harold's Plus 4 left the hospice gate as the Rally Instruction Book required, at precisely 9.35 a.m. and with Fred clearly calling, "Left turn 200 metres. Roundabout third exit 400 metres. Railway bridge, keep right," and all manner of route indications to the garden centre luncheon stop. Then through the scenic route back to the hospice for tea, arriving without losing the route over the whole 120 miles and getting the finishers' stamp and commemorative plaque exactly on time to the minute. Both driver and navigator shook hands over tea like a veteran rally team.

Over the next few months Harold found the occasional invitations to the Blake's most enjoyable and their acceptance of his return 'Pub Suppers', a highlight in his week. Enjoyment that was greatly enhanced by Fred's interest and active involvement in working on the Plus 4 highlighted by Harold's servicing of the Morgan's engine and clutch when Fred's help and interest was invaluable.

Several one day rallies for other charities in the area followed and on one famous event only three months to the day after Muriel had passed on, the Plus 4 Morgan with Harold driving and Fred navigating, were successful in winning the rally's 'Performance Award' cup for the most success points won over the day's event.

The Blakes were, understandably, proud of their son and most gracious about Harold's driving, so much so that the pub landlord provided a round of drinks for everyone in the place by way of congratulations. Fred went home with the cup as his proud possession and Harold walked back home, amazed to find Mrs Hilda Barnthorpe 'out of doors' watering the tub of pansies by her front door.

"Good evening, Mrs Barnthorpe. Lovely, it's still light at 10 o'clock." Harold said risking direct communication.

"Good evening, Mr Pilgrim, yes and well done today with that nice little car of yours and Mrs Blake's boy." And with that Mrs Barnthorpe retreated through her front door, with what might have been a smile, although Harold could not be quite sure in the gathering half-light.

Harold let himself into his own front door and went straight to the front room and opened the polished wooden desk, letting down the writing flap. "There we are, Muriel," he said, getting out the long brown envelope with the printed label 'Last Will and Testament, Harold Pilgrim, Esq.'

Drawing a sheet of headed notepaper from one of the cubicles in the open desk, sliding the wicker-backed chair into a position where he could write, he put pen to paper. "I know you will agree, Muriel, because thanks to your thoughtfulness and bothering about me when you had so much to think about, I feel I now have an extended family, and I know you will approve of this." Harold then wrote, clearly and precisely. "I leave my 1935 Morgan +4 MLL 22 together with all my tools and equipment to Frederick Blake, currently residing at No. 20 Clovelly Avenue. Further my estate will provide sufficient funds to rent a secure garage of his choice until Frederick is 21 years of age to house the +4 Morgan and all tools and equipment."

Harold signed and dated the authority and slid the paper into his will envelope before he went up to his bedroom and smiled as he looked up Clovelly Avenue in the gathering summer darkness.

A CAREER MOVE

I had never liked the sales manager and I was certain sure he had never liked me.

"Well, I am a little surprised you are looking for this transfer to HR at this point in your career." He looked up at me from the papers on his black, fake, leather desk top in the smarmy, smug 'I'm caring' way he had.

"It is," he continued, "unusual for someone who has spent the last, what is it, eight years in my sales area to move to a different department?"

'Of course it is, you fat, unpleasant idiot,' I thought, 'and you know damn well why I am going. I'm never going to get on the road as a field salesman under your lousy management appraisal system, and in a week's time I will hit the dreaded thirty mark, and will be permanently desk bound in my boring job.'

"Well, Sir," I said, "with your support I think I can move into the HR role with benefit from my experience in your department."

He shuffled his papers, no doubt thinking, 'If the rumours are correct, that's another one off my headcount for whom I don't have to pay redundancy!'

"Okay," he said, "I have signed the transfer. Keep your nose clean. I hope you can find your way about in all that red tape bull shit down there!"

At this point he closed the file abruptly and in his usual dismissive way, waved his hand towards the door.

'Thank goodness for that you fat idiot,' I thought as I went out of the door. Although the nagging anxiety about my imminent interview for the new role kept surfacing, as I went to collect the few personal items I kept in my desk by one of the windows in the corner of the sales office.

The nearest sales clerk, with a desk in front of mine, wheeled his overweight sweaty presence around to see me clearing out my desk. "It went well then," he said, sneering.

"Well, we had a good chat and he sees the logic of my career move and wished me well." I had rehearsed my speech carefully.

"I bet," he smirked, "he was delighted to get another body off his headcount without even trying."

"Well, see you around," I said without looking at him and I totally ignored the other four clerks as I walked out with a plastic bag of items, feeling rather than hearing their sniggers.

Walking home in teaming rain, it became clear to me that the Head of HR would know that my interest in a "career move" had been stimulated by my lack of success in getting on to the field force team and by a desire to retain a job, any job, in the upcoming, cost cutting, company exercise. He would know perfectly well that if I faced a job hunting exercise at the age of thirty, without any professional achievements in the depressed recruitment market, the result was likely to be that I would be lucky to find myself in the cab of a delivery van for the next few years.

These depressing, negative, thoughts were running through my mind as, dripping wet, I let myself into the third floor flat in the High Street tenement building, distinguished only by its Sixties architecture. As I had every day for the month since she had walked out, I saw her bright red umbrella in the mirrored hat stand, the only thing she had left behind as she swept out to "progress her life" which, as I recall her saying several times "has been going nowhere for far too long."

Analysing her departure as best I could in the depressing and I have to say, lonely hours I had spent since her departure, I had come to accept that my negative reaction to formalising the partnership, despite her mother's constant reference to 'us not getting any younger' and the girlfriends, all of whom seemed to be pushing prams or coyly sharing intimate details about their pregnancy conditions and their "pool birthing" plans, had not gone down well.

A negative response I can now reflect was based largely upon my own concerns about my frustration and growing belief that I was a professional failure at the age of thirty, left behind by the receding tide of success, who was most unlikely to be able to achieve the income to support a wife and family.

My own audit of personal performance, influenced by acknowledging the progress being made by several of my old school colleagues, whose sharp cars and 'trophy' wives loudly promoted their growing success and as I reflected upon the matter, gave me another reason why my circle of friends had declined so radically over the last three or four years.

"I am about to have an interview, leading to change in my job. On top of this," I said to my own reliable, and very regular confidant, the barman at the Royal Oak, "I realise I cannot afford to keep the flat now that she is not making a contribution, because even if I get the new job the wage grade is at least one level lower than mine, so I am going to have to give a month's notice to the landlord tomorrow."

He filled my depleted pint glass with the brewer's best bitter, without looking for payment and as often the way in the miserable November evenings, settled himself on his three-legged stool behind the beer taps where he could survey the length of the bar should a customer find the strength, or enthusiasm, to fight their way from the High Street through the wind and rain.

I had earlier even wondered about the short trip myself, barely one hundred yards from my tenement flat. More, of course, if you took the three flights of stairs into account, a thought that did not trouble me on the way to the pub, but occasionally weighed heavily on the return journey, the lift having been classed as 'off duty' ever since I had taken up residence.

"I could do with a bit of advice," I said, addressing my pint glass rather than the barman. He was by now well used to my release of office frustration in his direction on my regular visits on my way from work.

In the beginning I had seen this communication as a step to clear the air before I met my partner, so that I would not burden her with my frustrations.

When I had tried to explain my office circumstance, at least after the first month or so of our joint existence, I received very short shift and a "get a grip" or "well do something about it" was more often than not the response, hence my growing reliance upon the seemingly more understanding barman. Well, if not more understanding, at least with a vocabulary of nods, headshakes, and "unbelievable", more tolerant.

Now I needed some advice and, I reflected, probably from the only unbiased source I could consider sharing my professional predicament with. This thought departed as soon as it had registered, as I realised I was really being paralysed about my few-days-away thirties threshold, and my failure to make any mark in the world.

"I am going for a pee," I announced, unnecessarily, and he grunted an acknowledgement.

In fact I went to pass thoughts, not water, thinking out my request for 'advice' without overburdening the request to him with pointless detail, or in the frail emotional state I was in and bursting into tears as I described my situation.

I eyed my dishevelled appearance in the toilet mirror noticing, as always, the receding hairline. Deciding to concentrate only on two or three points looking for his advice, I returned to my stool and the half full beer glass. As far as I could see my bar friend was in exactly the same position he had been as I had left him.

"I would value your views as an experienced guy before I take on the interview tomorrow," I said, feeling a little sheepish.

In saying this I realised despite hours of casual chat about football, politicians, women, the weather etc., I really knew nothing about him, and now looking at him afresh he could be no more than a couple of years older than me, if that. Still, I had to share my anxiety with someone I trusted.

"I'm going for a job in HR as I am fed up with the sales office. You see lots of business guys in here. Got any tips for tomorrow's meeting?"

Sitting back and taking a pull at my beer, I reflected these were the facts and I had got the situation over quite clearly.

"What do HR people do?" he asked.

Somewhat confused I realised I only had a sketchy idea of what HR people actually did.

"Well you know, Human Resources, managing the payroll, I suppose, sorting out the salary grades – err – interviews for the new employees. I suppose making sure people are fired properly, you know that sort of thing," I blurted out.

The barman had swung round on his stool and was regarding me closely. I found this somewhat disconcerting but he said nothing for several minutes. Then he said, "You got a decent suit and tie?" as he continued to eye my dishevelled appearance. "You've time to pop into the little Italian barbers, 'Carlo's', on the corner. So, here's my advice, for what it's worth. Go home via the barber, look up HR services on the Web when you get home. Tomorrow wear your best suit and tie and be on time for the interview."

And with this said, he got up to serve a group of noisy and decidedly damp business guys straggling into the bar. No doubt looking for a booster for their journey home.

Carlo snipped and combed efficiently and turned off the lights and bolted the door as I left, collar up, hands into my pockets into the still raining night but with the thought that 'Step One' had been accomplished.

Back in the flat I Googled my way into Wikipedia.org and HR, techniques and management, scanning the copious range of headings and summaries, and data related to what I had previously thought to be the simple process of firing somebody, or making them redundant! My thinking being that if this issue was high on the HR manager's agenda, the more informed I sounded at my interview and the better my chance of being retained in work.

I soon found that the information on Performance Appraisal Techniques (P.A.T. as it was referred) became the focus of my attention, during which it dawned upon me that none of the 'key steps' had ever been applied in my case. 'Periodic process,' 'pre-established and agreed criteria', 'feedback to employees' were all contributions according to the website for a well-ordered employers' organisation. The detail of which read like a foreign language to me!

A sheaf of notes and eye watering awareness some time later, I crashed into bed, thinking 'Step Two' had been achieved.

Jerked awake by the alarm, after a sleep dominated by nightmare interviewers disparaging my desperate attempts to explain my potential for one job or another, I was pleased to find the value of rehanging my rather careworn suit the night before had eliminated most of the creases and my single silk tie with a matching top pocket handkerchief, unused since my aunt had gifted the set on a long forgotten birthday, seemed to fit the bill for today.

After a quick cup of coffee, being as much as I could manage, gulped down between my final audits of my appearance, I slammed the flat door and went out into a rather cold, grey looking day but at least with no rain.

Reading my HR notes proved rather difficult despite being locked on to a standing pole in the Underground amongst the going-to-work crush, and this decided me to use the notes openly as a reference in my interview in the hope, as I saw the matter, that would convince the HR manager that I had attempted a serious commitment to the subject.

I took a long walk, with my new haircut and old best suit, through the company's corridors to remain calm by avoiding old sales clerk colleagues, aiming to be on time for my 9.00 a.m. appointment with the HR manager in his prestigious front office. A strategy only slightly disturbed by one of my casual clerical acquaintances from the accounts department, who enquired politely as we passed, 'if I was on my way to a funeral'.

At 8.55 a.m. precisely I was ushered into the HR manager's impressive office, which I had never been privileged to enter before, despite my eight years in the company.

The HR manager stood up from his wide leather padded chair, with a broad white toothed smile and handshake, although his greeting was lost in the deluge of gurgling sounds emanating from the enormous drinking water dispenser situated an arm's length from his desk.

When the water dispenser eruption had subsided, the HR manager asked me to sit down, indicating one of the two chairs in front of his desk. I did so and immediately became aware that my seat was several inches lower than his. 'A creative dominant benign communication environment' referred to in my HR 'leadership' reading of last night!

"Now then," again the broad white tooth smile, which suggested an expensive relationship with a leading Harley Street dentist. "I understand you are keen to join the department?" This line was delivered with some emphasis that, I guess, Genghis Khan might have used to a warrior anxious to join his rampaging horde.

"Well, yes sir, I am very anxious to make a career move where I can gain … err … earn," I responded, "the opportunity to work more closely with people, well ...err... with our employees … people." I staggered to a halt.

He looked up from his desk "Now I see from your manager that you have had a fairly long period in the sales department?"

'Obviously that fat idiot is desperate to get rid of me,' I thought but continued, "Well, yes sir. I just feel I have more to offer in the HR field."

"Right, well you do understand there are several applicants from outside the company with suitable accreditation, which of course you do not have at this point…," here he shuffled his papers whilst reading some details, "and you do understand this is a lower grade level than you are currently on?" He added, "As the other applicants are all rather younger than you."

'Here we go again,' I thought, 'over the hill at thirty bullshit.'

At this point his secretary hurried into the room and, I thought, rather unceremoniously smacked a note in front of him, pointing a finger at the content.

The HR manager visually tightened up. "Good grief," he said, standing up. "Look just hang on here for a minute." No toothy smile now, as he rushed out with his secretary in close pursuit.

'Typical,' I thought, sitting back. 'No one in this bloody company gives a damn about my interests. Here I am, what, three days before my dreaded thirtieth birthday looking at a "No hope for the future" sign. I really would be better using my time to get down to the Job Centre where I can still sign in as twenty-nine!'

Standing up, I gathered my papers when one of the three phones on the desk, rang. The one with a little flashing red light on the top.

I stared at it and went round the desk and opened the secretary's door to find that room empty.

I returned to the HR manager's desk and picked up the receiver. "I'm sorry…" I was cut short by the voice of the company chairman, which I recognised having had to listen to his entreaties for more and greater endeavours every company Christmas lunch!!!

"There is a very important client," and the emphasis on "very" left no doubt that was the status, "being brought down to the HR office. Receive him politely and explain that I and the directors will be down in a minute or two, and for goodness sake say as little as possible." And with this said, the line went dead.

At the same moment the outer door opened and a girl I recognised from the company reception desk, made way for the entry of a large, rather portly, Asian man in an immaculate light grey double-breasted suit, a silk handkerchief in his top pocket, arranged not folded, and a matching silk tie. He was followed in by a small Asian man in a neat dark suit, holding a large crocodile briefcase.

The receptionist, head down, holding the door open, rather awkwardly curtsied her way out backwards.

Realising I had no option, I rounded the desk to stand in front of the imposing Asian gentleman. "Good morning, sir, would you and you're..." I tailed off as 'assistant' did not seem to fit the bill, "care to sit down," and I waved, I thought rather gracefully, to the large leather couch against the wall. "The chairman and directors will be with you – momentarily." I began and then realised I had used the word "momentarily" to add status to the invitation and was quite pleased with myself.

The imposing businessman did not sit down but said in impeccable English, "I have little time but no doubt you will be briefed on why I am here?" Fortunately he did not wait for my response, which was just as well as I did not have one. "My assistant, Mr Hakani, will be presenting the papers to your board."

At this point he looked around as if expecting the board to materialise from the carpet, and glanced at his heavy gold bracelet watch.

This exchange, one sided as it was, had at least given me time to recall something of the lead article in the company's employee newsletter that said, "A major international electronics group from Bangalore, India, is evaluating our company's progress to promote their..." I then seemed to remember their "revolutionary blue light" ... Diodas was it? ... Yes, LEDs. Miniature light bulbs. I also recalled the bulbs would radically reduce energy bills.

I unfroze significantly to say, "Well, if I can assist Mr Hakani in any way until the chairman and board arrive, I would be delighted to do so."

This offer seemed to trigger a decision in the great man's mind. He waved Mr Hakani forward with a manicured and ringed hand. "Be kind enough to give my assistant your name and extension details," he said.

Mr Hakani moved to the desk, opening his commodious briefcase as he did so. In heavily accented but perfect English he said, "If you would be kind enough to note down your details", sliding a plain pad emblazoned with the heading 'President Ajay P Shuira, Leading Edge Ultrasonic Corp. Bengaluru, India.

As I noted down my name, my mind racing, I thought it better in the circumstances not to write in my sales office telephone extension. I surreptitiously glanced at the three phones on the HR manager's desk, selecting the one with the red light button and marked with a direct line number, and copied this on to the pad.

"As President Shuira has an eleven o'clock appointment with the British Commissioner for Indian Business, a friend from his days at Oxford, I am afraid we will have to leave now," Mr Hakani said, looking up to President Shuira, who nodded. "If I may I will leave the proposal papers with you for your board, and if you could call me on my mobile." He passed me a business card embossed in gold with 'Leading Edge Ultrasonic Corp' and his name with the title 'Assistant to the President'.

"When your board would like to meet, President Shuira is staying at Claridges." Again he looked up at his President who nodded to the unspoken question. "We would like to liaise the meetings through you."

I felt a response was essential and introducing my entry with a slight cough, I said, "I hope you and the president will not mind if I mention the excitement that the opportunity to be … associated." I decided this was a safe word to use. I repeated it, "Associated with the revolutionary LED bulb developments of your great organisation."

Suddenly I felt I had overstepped the mark and my bold reference might have been for an LEM or was it LAM? I was therefore greatly relieved when the Chairman nodded an acceptance even, I thought, giving me a half smile.

This said, Mr Hakani retrieved a thin file of documents from the depths of the briefcase and handed it to me before closing the elegant clasp. "Now the car please."

I leaped into action, opening the door and leading the way to reception where an Indian driver in a smart grey uniform and peaked cap with 'Leading Edge Ultrasonic Corp' embroidered in gold on a pocket badge, swiftly opened the outer door to one huge black Rolls Royce as the rather short receptionist curtseyed and virtually disappeared behind the desk, catching I supposed the spirit of the event, whilst I held the company door as the visitors climbed into the rear seat luxury of the Rolls Royce.

I noted with some pleasure that I had done the right thing to bow my head as the car swept silently away as the president's hand raised an acknowledgement.

"Bloody hell," I said to the receptionist who had regained her stool and composure, "what a morning." She nodded and then said, "I think they are looking for you, they are all in the HR manager's office."

My head was spinning as I walked down the corridor but at the same time I felt elated by the whole event. My mind was churning. What should I do? I mean how should I play this strange event to the HR manager? Would it make any difference to my opportunity to hold on to a job in the company? I mean, I seemed to have played the cards alright as far as the Indians were concerned but then again had I? I could not really know and I might still be off to the Job Centre later today!

I opened the door into the HR manager's office to find a scene of considerable chaos.

Three of the six men in the room were on the phone. The chairman, who I recognised from the Christmas pep talks, was sitting in the HR manager's seat and on the phone with the red button. Two of the others, I assumed to be directors, were crouched on the long leather sofa on their mobiles with earnest, and I thought anxious expressions, their spare hands clamped over their free ear.

The other three were standing in the middle of the room, heads together, arguing about something without, I thought, seeming to be listening to each other's arguments.

My arrival at the door transformed the scene almost I thought standing there, as a change of act in a stage drama.

The chairman banged down the phone and shouted "Quiet", looking at me. The directors muttered quickly into their mobiles and switched off and the three stared at me silently. I realised I was still holding the thin proposal file of papers Mr Hakani had handed me.

The chairman rose and transformed his features into his 'be at ease with your leader' role. "Come in, please. Sit down," and he swept to the other side of the desk, waving me to one of the chairs as he took the other.

"Now," he said, "would you be kind enough, in your own time, to fill the board in with what happened when you met President Shuira and Mr—?"

"Mr Hakani," I interjected.

"Yes of course," the chairman said, "Mr Hakani."

The board had gathered, standing around the HR manager's desk. Staring at me, it seemed to me, as if I was the Christmas turkey at the company lunch.

"Well, sir," I said, suddenly realising that I might indeed have an HR job opportunity negotiating position if I played my cards right. "President Shuira did suggest ... to me," I added, "that he would like a fairly...," here I took a risk, "fairly quick response to his proposals."

"Exactly," one of the directors exploded. I think he was the administration director. "If finance had done their job, and sorted the numbers, we would have been in negotiations right now." He said this glaring at the finance director on the other side of the desk.

This interjection caused a chorus of complaint and counter challenge, until the chairman banged the table. "For goodness sake, don't start all that again. Let's hear what Mr…" he tailed off and I realised neither he nor any other member of the board knew my name and it was now clearly an awkward moment to ask me.

"Could you please continue," he said to me, putting on his 'complete confidence in you' smile.

"Well, sir," I said, sliding the file towards him. "Mr Hakani did imagine I had some … err … understanding of the programme." At this point my stumbling dissertation was stopped by the white phone on the desk, bleeping. The chairman picked it up and shot to his feet, or at least rose briskly for a man of his bulk. "Of course put him through … Mr Hakani how nice to hear from you, I am so sorry…" At this point he tailed away. Then he said "Of course, one of our brightest young men … I quite agree a most suitable liaison for you … did the president indeed. Well we like to think we give our top young men every opportunity. Yes, thank you so much, we will certainly follow the programme as you suggest and deal with the matters outstanding as a matter of urgent priority."

He then looked at the receiver which had clearly gone dead. His gaze gradually came back into focus as he surveyed the silent room. I had been thinking intently during his telephone exchange.

True, I was now motivated by the unexpected opportunity this surprising morning suggested and reflecting it was only, and I glanced at my watch, two hours and thirty minutes ago that I was sitting in this same seat, nervously hoping I could somehow get a pathetic, badly paid job here, as an alternative to being made redundant.

But what was really burning me up was the chairman's reference to "bright young men in our top team, giving them every opportunity."

What a load of rubbish! I had been shouted at or ignored by that fat idiot in the sales office. Every application I had ever made over eight years had been turned down, or ignored, and the slimy HR manager was clearly never going to take me on to his headcount.

The chairman looked at me and said, "Well done, it seems we have saved the day. Now if we could work out an immediate plan of action based, of course, on Mr Hakani's … err … suggestions."

Quite suddenly my script fell into place as clearly as if I was reading it on my not very up to date laptop screen. I stood up. "I am sorry gentlemen, I really have to leave. I have an appointment in an hour and I really cannot afford to miss the opportunity. You may not have realised that as of this morning I am no longer employed in your sales office, and my earlier interview with your HR manager gave me no indication that a suitable role was open to me in this department."

I then moved towards the door. The chairman looked as if he was imminently about to suffer a heart attack and the board members had all taken on the facial expressions of individuals who had quite recently been involved in a car crash.

The chairman recovered sufficiently to cut off my walk to the door and he took my arm. "I quite understand," he said. "A man of your ability must do the best for himself, but could I ask you to give me … the company, just a few more minutes." At this point he was clearly pleading.

Still holding my arm he walked me down the corridor and asked the receptionist to get his secretary to come down – immediately. She materialised magically only moments later. "Mr…," and he coughed politely, "has kindly agreed to give us a few moments of his time. Please take him to the Executive Entertainment Suite for a few minutes and get the HR manager to my office". He delivered the last part, I thought, with something of an edge.

His quite comely secretary wafted me into the executive lift and into the innermost sanctuary of the top floor, where apparently I could avail myself of any one of the world's range of whiskies including, I noted, those brewed in India. Or any other beer or alcoholic beverage, from anywhere. I settled for a coffee – black, and she dematerialised leaving me with the perfumed impression that her perfect smile and couture suit were somehow still in the room.

I decided I had played my cards right and perhaps, just perhaps, my very nearly thirty years of experience had for the first time really been of value in reacting to the ebb and flow of the morning's amazing events.

I looked in the elegant mirror, flanked by historic company photos of the directors and their business guests at golf events, seeing myself for the first time in a positive light without my reflection burdening me with doubt and anxiety.

The chairman's secretary materialised again, holding open a door that was cleverly designed to look like part of the bookcase with rows of bound company records, for the chairman followed by an extremely harassed looking HR manager.

"Gerald," the chairman trumpeted. So he had finally got my name! "I do hope we haven't held you up too long."

Without looking at the HR manager, he waved a hand in his direction and the manager passed a single sheet of paper to him. "Could we sit for a minute?"

He pulled out a high-backed polished wooden seat from the circular table in the middle of the room, waiting for me to sit down before he joined me, whilst the HR manager hovered anxiously in the background.

"Gerald," he said, "I do apologise that we have not had time to put together a contract but I have had the directors offer a key senior management position typed out for you to consider before your next interview." He slid the single sheet of paper across the table to me.

Composing my features in my newly found 'thespian' roles to 'calm and indifference' I read the job proposal, and very nearly fluffed the lines. The 'Co-ordinating Administrative Manager' was not entirely surprising but the salary, some three times my existing plus an annual performance bonus was, had I allowed it to be, an eye opener.

But what very nearly shocked me into expressing surprise, was the clause that would require regular visits, travelling business class, to India plus a company car.

"Of course," the chairman said, "you would be reporting directly to me on this, the most important programme the company has ever had and you will need a personal assistant to cover for when you travel etc. Perhaps you know a suitable candidate you would like to bring in, at whatever salary you think appropriate," he added. "If you could let us know if you can accept the proposal later today, I will have a contract ready for you to sign, and of course your new office in the executive suite made ready".

It was just twelve o'clock by the clock in the empty bar as I wandered in, still reeling from the size and scope of my new job proposal.

"How did the interview go?" queried the barman as he automatically pulled me a pint of best bitter. "How would you like a new job, Joe?" I replied.

COMMUNICATING WITH THE ENEMY

My dad drew the Ford Prefect to a halt right by the entrance to the station. I pushed the passenger door open carefully, holding on to my canvas holdall which I had perched on my lap.

I held the door open as my mother tipped the passenger seat forward and climbed with a little difficulty from the back seat, stepping carefully over the high door sill as she did so.

We both knew how particular my dad was about the high state of polish he had in his pride and joy, the black nine horse power motor vehicle, both inside and out, so all chips or scratches were carefully avoided!

We stood a little awkwardly under the station entry sign. My mother was trying but failing to hold back her tears as she gave me a long hug. "Now, mind you have your sandwiches," she said, "on that long journey."

I felt choked but managed to say, "Course I will, Mum," as I untangled myself.

Dad held out his hand as he said, "Now you look after yourself, son. Remember what I told you last night."

To be honest I could not remember too much about our conversations after consuming several pints with him, topped by a large malt whisky, a tipple that did not generally come my way!

I did remember several incidents being recounted of his Air Sea Rescue experiences, particularly picking up downed pilots in the English Channel during the Battle of Britain period. The stories I had heard since I was a lad, and the reason after all I had gone for the RAF, but the 'don't do this', 'watch your backside if this happened etc.', rather passed me by, well intentioned though I knew them to be.

Dad shook my hand firmly, and said, "Now make sure you phone your mother when you arrive." He then thrust an envelope into my hand and climbed back into the Ford with a "Come on mother or he will miss his train" and with that the shiny little black car was driving out of the station yard.

I stared at the envelope that was not stuck down. There were five one pound notes inside. I could scarcely believe it, a month's money from my miserable office job all in my hand. Slipping the fortune into my leather wallet which had two shillings and six pence in the attached purse, I felt suddenly ready to take on the world.

I marched up to the ticket inspector at the concertinaed metal gate barrier. An imposing figure in his black uniform and shiny peak cap, who in normal circumstances would cause me some anxiety as his scrutiny suggested you were trying to get on to the train without paying, or at the very least, take a ticket for a shorter train journey than you intended.

The ticket inspector looked down his bespectacled nose as he took my buff National Service travel document and clipped the required section for train and bus travel to RAF Henley. "Good luck to you, son," he said and smiled at me to the considerable surprise of the two elderly ladies standing behind me, waiting to have their cardboard tickets clipped.

The inspector then said authoritatively, "You'll find your train on Platform 3," and he glanced at the large station clock just behind him. "In seven minutes."

I thanked him politely, feeling rather grown up and marched up the wooden steps and across the bridge to Platform 3.

"Six one, thirty seven, thirty six, sixteen tens...," the staff sergeant barked out my statistics to his clerk, scribbling my kit sheet, who was judging everything by eye as I shuffled by in the long line of National Service entrants moving along the line of supply airmen clerks, each with a long trestle table with best blue jackets, best blue trousers, working blue jackets, working blue trousers, shirts, pants, socks, belts, braces, boots. The line of supply benches in the cavernous warehouse stretched on for ever.

The first clerk, who had ticked the basic physical dimensions in each box on the sheet, handed me my sheet recording the sizes shouted out by the staff sergeant and I shuffled on in the queue.

"Next," was called out, and the pile of clothes became larger in my arms with the words 'Sports shorts and two sports shirts'. Then with the usual military efficiency, the next station was 'Kit bags' so that all the soft clothes were dumped in before the heavy 'Great Coat', that of course had to be put on, and boots were collected.

Back in the billet, like everyone else, I was given 'ten minutes' to check that the sizes all fitted. "Get it wrong you horrible airmen and that collar will throttle you for the next two years," said the corporal.

The collection of items from darning bits to mess tins seemed endless and the induction process, including how to pack, wear and carry the prescribed Royal Air Force support equipment was enough to make my head throb and by day three I could scarcely remember if I had ever had a home, and if I had where it was!

31

On Day three at 6.00 a.m. we were advised there would be interviews and according to the list on the board at the end of my billet …. '2589008 F. Butt was required to be present at the Interview Centre, Block 12, Cubicle B, with All Academic, Craft and work related Certification at 8.55 a.m. for the initial Trade Interview with Flight Lieutenant Hamilton'.

I duly found myself in my working blue uniform with my size 10 very uncomfortable boots, seated on a wooden bench outside the curtained Cubicle B at 8.45 a.m. with a slight case of indigestion having gulped down breakfast and run from the canteen, so as not to be late.

My preparation, rehearsed in my mind several times, was somewhat disrupted by the interview in front of mine. I could hear the voices loud and clear and the listening did not help my self-confidence. "Jones,' came the loud voice of the interviewer, "I do realise you have three School Certificate passes in, let's see, Geography, History and English but two Bs and a D does not constitute a sufficient academic standard for me to recommend you to be considered for the Education corps."

Jones piped up. "But, sir, when I get back into Civvy Street I'm going to be a teacher."

"Well, Jones, I can only hope that will be in woodwork, but in the meantime I can only propose you as a useful candidate for a 'General Duties' role in the RAF," continued the officer in a monotone voice.

"But, sir…"

"Thank you, Jones 932, that will be all. – Next."

Sitting looking at the file in front of him on his grey steel service desk with a small stand up label proclaiming 'Duty Officer Flt.Lt. M.B. Hamilton' the officer said, "Well, Butt 008, what branch of our service do you feel you wish to spend the next two years engaged in?"

"Air Sea Rescue service, sir," I was able to promptly reply.

"I see,' said Flt.Lt. Hamilton, "and why the interest?"

"Well, sir, my dad was a Coxswain Flight Sergeant during the War based in Dover Marina, picking up downed pilots, sir."

"Was he indeed? Do you know what boats he was on?"

I was able to respond, enthusiastically now. "Yes, sir, Thorneycroft Beetlebacks they called them. Twin Merlin engines, carrying supplementary ack-ack, built at the Swan Hunter yard, sir."

"Well, Butt, you clearly know what you are talking about and so I am going to pass you on to the officer dealing with Special Service intake. Now I see he will not be interviewing until Thursday and so you go and cool your heels until 8.45 a.m. Thursday morning. Back here then to see," and he studied another list he had, "Flt.Lt. Gore. Off you go."

The days dragged by, trapped in the Intake Entry camp, whilst the rest of my intake departed to the Square Bashing camp for the required eight weeks.

My interview with Flt.Lt. Gore was short, sharp and disappointing. "I understand, Butt, you wish to join the Air Sea Rescue Service. You may do so provided you sign on for five years," he said.

"Oh no, sir, not me, sir, I'm National Service," I replied.

"Well, Butt, if you are not prepared to sign on I shall assign you for 'General Duties' and," he then checked another list, "you will do your initial training at Wilmslow, Manchester. Collect your travel vouchers at admin and travel tomorrow."

"Sir," I said as I saluted and went out.

Arrival at the Wilmslow Guard House and passing over my travel and assignment papers filled me with apprehension. The guard house was the largest I had seen and the duty sergeant did not help by saying, "Well, Butt, you are going to be lonely until next Monday when the next intake comes in. The camp was cleared yesterday after the service's squads for the Royal Tournament finished training and went down to London, so you have the camp to yourself until Monday. You're in Hut 118, right out of the guard house and keep walking."

Manchester in March was not kind and with my great goat collar up and my kit bag heavy on my shoulder, I finally found Hut 118.

Twenty beds, each with a wooden side cabinet, and an RAF grey tin clothes locker between each bed.

I stood dismally surveying the scene, when the door at the top of the hut opened and a corporal came in. "You, what are you doing here?" he shouted.

"I don't know, sir, I was just sent", proffering my papers.

"Not sir, say Corporal when you address me."

"Yes, Corporal," I replied quickly.

"Now you better explain why you are here. Hang on, wait a minute," and to my considerable surprise he disappeared into his room and came back out with two mugs of tea. "Ok, you take the bed here by my door and dump your stuff on the bed for a mo. Now tell me why you have turned up before the other 99 of your intake?"

I went through the whole reason for getting out of step.

Corporal Harry Beaumont, after he had said, "Bad luck", explained he was waiting for an overseas posting and had been 'dumped' on to this intake square bashing assignment whilst his own assignment came through and it was clear he was a long way from being pleased.

The now relaxed discussion threw up that our families lived barely ten miles apart and better still, we both supported the same football team.

Corporal Harry said, "Look I will show you round and give you the drill for this place, cause it's loaded with bull here, and you can then help me when the new intake arrive on Monday. They wander around not knowing Christmas from Easter and you can show 'em the ropes because I'm all for a quiet life and every intake is different – right! I'm, just hanging on until my posting comes through. Incidentally, Flight Sergeant Blake is the Senior NCO for the intake and he hates National Service men, with a passion."

"Yes, Harry, eh Corporal," I blurted out.

"Keep it to corporal when anyone's around. Okay? Keep your nose clean and well away from Flt.Sgt. Blake. Okay?" he stressed, looking at me sharply.

The corporal's instructions were also very specific about the 'Do's and Don'ts' to avoid doing a stretch of 'Jankers' under the eye of the 'Goons'. Words I had not come across in my civvy life covering breaking service rules and the Military Police. Bending rules, such as from leaving your top button undone to dropping a fag butt or walking through an area designated as an officers' corridor was, I thought, a 24/7 nightmare to avoid, as I desperately tried to remember the instructions I was getting.

I realised Corporal Harry was instructing me for his own interests but our relationship had, I thought, stabilised fairly early once it dawned on me he was only a couple of years older than me and his experience would save me time and pain, so I took everything in from getting my boot toe caps up to the bull standard demanded by heating your mess spoon under the cast iron coke heater in the middle of the hut. Smearing boot wax liberally on the toe cap and working it in with the back of a hot spoon, I quickly found was the way.

The only drawback to having my bunk next to the corporal's room was the distance between me and the only heating that was smack in the middle of the hut!

Boot polish, Brasso to keep the military belt buckles shiny bright, Blanco to ensure the webbing was snow white, anything down to needles, cotton and replacements for missing buttons were to be had at the NAFFI in the centre of the deserted camp. This, along with any food the twenty-six shillings a week would stretch to after I had acquired the basic list of 'must have' items detailed by Corporal Harry, who several times favoured me with a mug of tea and a biscuit from his well-stocked bunk room, as we discussed the good and bad of our favoured football team as the hours dragged over the weekend.

The Sunday service that I was required to attend in the camp chapel, having registered C of E on my entrance papers, was only populated with drill sergeants and corporals and corporal P.T.I.'s. All, I thought, anxious to cause pain and suffering to the intake for eight weeks to whip a bunch of 'mummy's boys' into a fighting unit of the RAF.

In the billet just back from breakfast on Monday morning, the hut was invaded by nineteen brand newly uniformed young men with their shiny white kit bags, who crowded through the door in a noisy mob to be met head on by the hut corporal shouting and yelling at the top of his considerable voice, so that I lost all recognition of him as he indicated with a drill stick the men to their prescribed beds, before nineteen men and I formed two lines of ten on the edge of the parade ground in front of the hut. Without inclining my head from a rigid 'eyes to the front' position, I sensed another eighty National Service men, twenty to a hut, stood to attention along the parade ground.

Flt.Sgt. Blake stood in the centre of the parade ground with his team of drill instructors and each unit corporal faced his squad as Flt.Sgt. Blake barked out instructions and threats at the top of his considerable voice.

One hundred men were then instructed to store and stack their kit back in their bed space and lay out all their personal effects for an inspection. Immediately following the inspection, there would be the first eight mile route march.

The first shock of the many I was to get, back in the billet hut, was the fact that although I strained to hear what the discussions between the nineteen was about, I could not understand a single word.

I could understand being ignored after they had all been together at the RAF kitting out unit for several days but being ignored as if I wasn't there, what was all that about?

Within twenty minutes I had the next shock.

The Flt.Sgt. and a squad of corporals swept in to review the stored bedside cabinets and the tallboy metal cupboards for each airman for correct storage and tidiness. Also looking through all the personal effects that lay out on the individual's bed.

The hut went silent when Flt.Sgt. surveyed the airman's bunk next to mine, a man I had not exchanged any communication with. "Hallo, what's this, a cyclist?" boomed the Flt.Sgt. holding up a highly polished cycle chain that was neatly coiled in amongst the airman's few personal effects. Flt.Sgt. wrapped the chain round the knuckles of his large right hand and stood very close to the airman, looking down on him as he said, "Airman, I know in Glasgow Gorbals you all go shopping with a chain just in case there is trouble, which there is frequently, so I'm not surprised I have confiscated eight chains already, and expect more, but in the Royal Air Force the only threats you will receive will be from the Military Police and I assure you, you would not wish to be found with one of these by one of them!!" This said, with a casual glance over my bed and cupboards, he swept out to the next hut.

Even though I could not understand the heavy dialect, other than occasional words within the crescendo of aggressive conversation he left behind, it was abundantly clear that being in the RAF was deeply resented and being in England was disliked even more, and having to take criticism from the NCOs was hated.

I remained as far away as the situation allowed and counted myself fortunate that I was simply ignored as I prepared for the first route march.

At 7.30 a.m. the next morning billet corporals, including Corporal Beaumont, shouted and aggressively screamed instructions to a scarcely awake and intimidated group of new National Servicemen, many struggling with tired limbs and aches and pains, as I did, from the previous day's route march.

Lined up in the early spring morning chill, the five hut corporals shouted out the names and the last three service numbers of various individuals, commanding, "One pace forward", bringing them clear of their other hut members.

The unfortunates were directed to the centre of the parade ground where the Squad Flt.Sgt. instructed them to "strip to your underwear". The uniforms were then collected and put to one side.

"You men failed to take a shower this morning." Clearly the hut corporals had watched over their required daily procedure with eagle eyes this morning.

Flt.Sgt. Blake shouted, "Right" and two Corporals holding the end of a fire hose, with a third turning the stopcock on the edge of the parade square, blasted cold water at the unfortunate eight.

After several uncomfortable minutes the water was turned off. The bedraggled airmen were directed to collect their uniforms and dress for breakfast.

Flt.Sgt. Blake then announced, I thought quite unnecessarily, that any airman caught dodging a morning shower would be subject to a naked scrub down with yard brooms on the square.

It was a very quiet breakfast that morning.

The days passed in a blur of twelve hour drill, march, climb, PT, rifle practice, all designed to exhaust and crush into conformity one hundred eighteen year olds.

The process did nothing to reduce the Scots' deep resentment to being at RAF Wilmslow and despite my inability to understand their language, particularly as I was very careful to keep well out of the way of the nineteen in my billet, and indeed the other eighty Glaswegians wherever it was possible to do so.

I had not had a conversation with a single serviceman by Friday morning of the first week of square bashing.

Corporal Beaumont had found the occasion, between shouting at nineteen recruits unwilling to carry out orders without the fear that there would be severe penalties if they did not, to give me the unhappy news that I was the lone Englishman with ninety-nine Scots from Glasgow's south bank of the Clyde River, Govan district and the Gorbals, and since each of them resented being in the RAF and hated the English "I better watch my backside". As if I didn't already know!

Just before the lunch break on Friday, with everyone changing after three hours of being goaded across the assault course, that had included grovelling along on my stomach whilst live 303 bullets were fired over my head, 'just over' was my state of mind, as I clung on to the muddy track, the postal clerk clattered through the billet throwing letters on the beds in response to his shouted names and the response 'Here'.

I had three letters, the first seen since leaving home, with my mother's hand, my sister's scrawl and an aunt's carefully cheerful words. The welcome arrival of the letter and their content brought a little reminder of home and real world into the prison-like atmosphere which I had to endure.

I finished sitting on my 'pit' and happened to glance at the Scot next to me, also sitting on his bed and apparently reading his single letter. Some second instinct told me he was not reading the single page.

I had not exchanged a single word with this dour Scot from Monday to Friday. Now, without looking his way I said over the side of my mouth, "Want me to read your letter?"

There was no immediate response. Then, quite suddenly, he slid the single page across his bed towards mine. Still looking directly at my locker I reached over and slid his letter into my own little pile.

Still looking forward and speaking slowly out of the side of my mouth, I read the brief letter from his mother expressing the desire he was eating proper food and she was missing him, all neatly handwritten with the address at the top of the sheet.

I slid the page back without any acknowledgement coming from the Scot.

That evening there was a single sheet of paper and an envelope on the top of my bedside locker.

Adopting the same procedure as we were both sitting on our beds, I enquired what he wanted to say to his mother. My side of the mouth question elicited a shrug of shoulders, and so I wrote the same letter that I had just written to my own mother. In the absence of knowing the Scot's first name, I put 'From your loving son', and having penned the address on the envelope, licked the envelope adhesive and dropped the letter on his bunk, I went to complete my ablutions for the night.

The transformation of my relationship with the Scots was extraordinary, all emanating from this simple act. Within a couple of days Scots were engaging me in conversations I could understand, and I responded equally carefully whenever I was addressed.

By the end of the next week I was the 'go to' airman when any Scot had concerns or needed some simple guidance on RAF procedure and in this matter Corporal Beaumont had picked up very quickly the extraordinary change in my role, and had clearly realised his and the other corporals' lives were much easier if the Scots had an English 'reference' man to go to, so he filled in any detail I was short on and my after supper NAAFI briefings to individuals became a regular event. I soon had a small group of 'non-readers' who came to rely upon my interpreting their home letters.

I also found for convenience that my single page weekly letter to my mother filled the bill for all the other mothers' letters. I expect my mother would have been surprised occasionally by my subjects!

In the seventh week of our incarceration the requirement under National Service procedure, was for each hut to put forward one of the twenty men to represent them at the final parade, presided over by the Commanding Air Officer.

The single choice from the five hut representatives was then decided upon by the drill and hut corporals and agreed by Flt.Sgt. Blake, for the airman to collect the Passing-Out Certificate and be the 'lead out' man for the parade.

I was sitting on my bed when Corporal Beaumont came in and said "Butt, get down to the NCO mess. There is a meeting and Flt.Sgt. Blake wants to see you – NOW, airman."

I stood to attention before the entire NCOs for the Flight Squad. "Butt," said Flt.Sgt. Blake, sitting against the NCO bar on a high three-legged stool. "Never in my years of dealing with you horrible National Service men have I come across a situation where every hut proposes the same man as the Squad No.1 Recruit." He looked at me quizzically.

I looked at the beer taps and said nothing.

"As you are the only Englishman in this intake and you cannot have bribed all the Scots, they must want you to have the honour!!!" Flt.Sgt. Blake continued. "So, Butt, you are the No. 1 Recruit and will collect the Passing-Out Certificate next week on behalf of the squad. Corporal Beaumont is of the opinion that when you get back to Civvy Street, you will become a lawyer, or a trade union leader, and I am inclined to agree. This being the case I have adjusted your next RAF training posting from the 'General Duties' depot you were going to go, to the RAF Education Training Centre where, I have no doubt, they will find ways to help develop your skill." With that he said, "In the meantime here is a pint to celebrate and well done young man and good luck for whatever you finally become."

GETTING THE PRIORITIES RIGHT

The plane's outer link with the airport was cut off abruptly with the clunk of the door shutting as the air hostess fussed me into the only remaining seat, mentioning my name several times whilst smiling at me before she fitted my Gucci briefcase into the locker above and closed it up.

I closed my eyes for a moment, trying to relax but this only made the excited mention of my name from the passengers behind more audible, and I was so pleased to observe I had no one in front of me staring and sharing the excitement of my presence with their friends.

This thought made me look to my right, initially across my immediate passenger's head, to see a middle aged, grey-haired lady who appeared at least to be asleep, with her head virtually on the elliptical window.

The thought process was broken by the young girl sitting between us, whose face was upturned towards me. "My auntie is scared of flying," she said without ceremony, clearly not expecting a response, and I was grateful to feel she had no idea – or interest in – who I was.

My attention was diverted as the pilot on the loudspeaker announced, "Please watch your air hostess who is now indicating your nearest escape exit." The hostess ignored company rules sufficiently to give me a warm smile as she stood almost in front of me with her arms wide.

Normally this excited some interest in me and the occasional long haul stopovers had, on occasions, resulted in convivial evenings in far flung airport hotels. However, today any thought of social intimacy was completely off my agenda.

Indeed, as the plane gathered height the only thought I had was the captain's confident assertion that the flight would only require an hour of his trained expertise. One hour, I realised, to sort myself out and prepare for the waiting television and press interviews.

Preparing, I thought bitterly, without the slightest assistance from my manager whose almost hysterical comments to me over the phone when I shared the news with him, only two hours ago, had, I now realise, been entirely driven by his own interests.

When I think how many millions that "blood sucker" had made from me in the two years since I had become World Champion and held that title, despite the intense competition from top players from every leading squash playing country around the world. To say nothing of the time I spend working to schedules for the lucrative sponsorship contracts, and holding down my working role as anchorman in the 'I am a World Champion' TV Sports programme that was about to go coast to coast prime time weekly with CMM. Even if, I thought depressingly, I am no longer the anchorman.

Now his instruction of "Hold off – say nothing about this. I am sure there is something we can do medically. I will get the best people on it – leave it to me. Do your thing, spin the press around your finger, you won't believe the CMM contract I am getting sorted for you."

All of this as I think back to his indifference to my news based upon his percentage interests in me as a money making resource.

The "Would you like tea or coffee and a light snack?" intoned close to my ear by the air hostess leaning over her trolley, snapped me into reality.

"Err, water please," I replied as she gave me a biscuit in a plastic packet and a smile with the bottle of water, before offering the same service to the small passenger next to me, having failed to raise any interest from the sleeping aunt, still curled awkwardly against the window.

When a drink of Coke in a plastic cup was dispensed with a biscuit to the little girl, I raised myself from despondency sufficiently to offer my packet biscuit to her. An offer that was accepted without comment, but with a beaming smile which quite transformed her pale small face with its frame of dark curly hair away from its serious, even anxious, look.

The dazzling smile caused me to quite involuntarily smile back at her. A light relief before I looked ahead to the impersonal brown plastic dividing barrier in front of my seat and concentrated my thoughts upon the event to come at the end of the journey.

Could I, the world No.1 squash player, who the gathered press expected would declare my intention to defend the title again next month and not only that but for a record third time in Dubai, at the same time announce the new USA CMM contract for the prime time TV show as the anchorman in the 'I am a Champion' sports programme.

How could I, how should I, announce my intentions?

Should I do as my manager wished and trumpet the next stage of my career, relying upon his assurances that he can smooth away my medical problems and all will be well?

Or should I now declare the depressing news given to me by my specialist only hours ago. "I am afraid the MRI clearly indicates the need to replace your left hip if you are not to suffer longer term physical damage caused by your present level of body balance that can often result in the need to replacement of the knee joint, in your case the right knee joint. Particularly so in your case with the required harsh training and playing you undertake, intermittent with your TV activities with periods of sedentary seated time not helping pressure on your damaged hip joint."

I then recalled the specialist continued with a lengthy diatribe on a theme over which he clearly was exercised: that of professional sports men and women who put their bodies under intense stress, resulting in ankle, knee, hip, back and shoulder damage, incidents of which he and his team are seeing more and more.

Whilst I had not been listening overly hard, being focused upon my own problems, I did remember his personal view that much of the problem could be traced to the professional trainees and team management pushing the sports stars to greater endeavours.

I realised I was no further forward towards the decision I have to come to on this flight about the statement I have to make, one way or another, in a couple of hours from now.

I have to unclutter my mind and find a way of not stressing myself so that I can think clearly.

At this point I became aware that the little girl's aged aunt was addressing me, having unhitched herself from the plane's window.

"Thank you for giving my niece your biscuit," she said politely.

I was pleased to see she had no recognition in her eyes as she addressed me a 'TV personality'! Indeed, I reflected on her neat, if a little worn, grey old fashioned jacket with small silver brooch fastening the collar at the neck. I supposed her interests would not have stretched to TV sports shows of any type.

At this point her niece addressed me for the first time. "Do you like flying on a plane?"

The matter came more in the form of a demand than a question.

"Well, not especially. I have to travel quite a lot so a plane helps me get about," I uttered.

"I have never travelled in a plane before but I like it. My aunt has never been in a plane before and she doesn't like it," was her response.

I was struck by the serious way these comments were made and by her close focus upon my face as she said them.

Having no children of my own, and I thought rather bitterly, only having girlfriends who regarded having children as an unacceptable barrier to their modelling careers, I had to struggle a little to find suitable words in which I might engage in some form of communication with this rather intense little girl.

I decided any interlude that would help me stabilise my thinking and help me to make a decision, was worth a try.

"Are you going to see some of your family?" seemed an appropriate start.

There was a pause, during which I noted the aunt had found the airline magazine and was thumbing through the ads, busily waiting for a reply.

Once again, I was struck by the penetrating gaze before she said, "No, I am going to an important meeting."

The mature and serious way this information was delivered, both interested and intrigued me. "Why, I am also going to a meeting – well an important meeting".

Just how important the meeting I thought was yet to be decided, but in any case it was certain to be life changing.

"I am going to see a real specialist," she said, "and everyone in my village – well nearly everyone, is interested."

"Goodness me that sounds very important," I said, somewhat surprised by the news. "I hope you and your aunt enjoy the meeting."

"I don't suppose I will," she said. "Actually I am a bit scared."

I struggled to find a suitable way to couch the next question. I need not have bothered.

"Everyone – well nearly everyone in the village, collected the money so I could fly in the plane and my aunt too."

She dropped her voice and squiggled closer on her seat towards me.

"My mum hasn't got any money, well not much anyway, and she got to look after the other kids, so she couldn't come."

Now fully focused on the small person beside me, I said, "Well, I expect the specialist will be a big help and not be scary at all."

The little girl's measured calm response was frightingly precise. "I have a special macular degeneration," she said this slowly as if she had practised several times, "and the optometrist told my mum that one day I won't be able to see at all. Well that is unless the man at the Moorfields Eye Hospital thinks I am ok to be used on a trial for a new drug."

"Even if this man says I am suitable, it's going to take lots and lots of money and my mum hasn't got much money. So I don't know how things will work out for me."

I struggled to say anything at all as I looked down at her beautiful expressive eyes and found myself very close to tears. What on earth was I feeling sorry for myself about?

Blowing my nose noisily, I realised an explanation of my own "important" meeting was called for.

"Your meeting is much more important than mine," I said to her. "I am seeing a load of journalists, well just sports journalists, as I have decided…," and at that second the right way forward was suddenly clear to me. I continued, "I have decided to retire from professional sport as I play quite a lot of squash. Do you know what that game is?"

"Oh yes," was the prompt reply. "It's just like tennis in a room with a rubber ball, so you don't have to keep picking up the ball." "Or," she said, "I suppose losing it, like at golf – but I suppose it gets a bit boring standing there with the ball bouncing around the walls all the time. Is that why you are stopping?"

I was suddenly forced to stop for a moment by her comment. Was I getting bored with the whole squash circus, all the training and hype?

However, I replied to her, "Well no, I have a bit of a problem with my hip which the doctor wants to take out and put in a metal one instead."

She looked surprised. "Metal, that sounds awful. Will you clank as you walk?" She laughed and then said, "I hope the man at Moorfields isn't thinking about replacing my eyes with metal ones, even if they do work!"

Slightly shocked by her thinking, I said, "Of course he won't. You will be getting eye drops, and what not, so your very nice eyes will just keep working."

"When they have replaced my hip joint I will certainly not be clanking, but I will have to give up a job on TV in a sports programme."

"You are on TV? How exciting," she said. "Are you in a soap or something?"

"No, sorry," I replied, "it's just a sports channel but I need to be playing squash successfully to stay in the TV programme, so it's time to move on. Do some new things."

"How exciting. Have you decided what new things you are going to do?" she enquired.

"Well not yet but I am getting together some ideas," I replied.

"Perhaps," she said enthusiastically, "you will get a part in a soap and I will be able to see you again." And her face lit up with her remarkable smile.

The hotel venue for the press and TV interviews was buzzing with rumours and counter-rumours when I and my small party arrived, an hour later than scheduled. I carefully got my guests seated before I moved to the stand of microphones at the lectern and the TV cameras switched to their bright "ON CAMERA" lights.

"Ladies and gentlemen. I do apologise for the delay in getting here but I had a very important appointment which I will explain to you in a minute, but before I do so I wish to announce that I will not be defending my World Championship title this year and I will explain why later. As a result I will be standing down as lead anchor in the "I am a Champion" show. However, I am proud to announce the show is going prime time coast to coast in the USA with CMM."

I waited whilst the hubbub of comment and exclamation that reverberated around the room following my announcements had somewhat abated.

"Now ladies and gentlemen, to what I regard as the important issues for me today. I would like to introduce an important young lady and her auntie," and I turned and extended my arm towards the little girl sitting almost lost in the high backed chair next to her aunt.

"Geraldine." And with the introduction her face transformed with her radiant smile, as cameras clicked and journalists pushed and shoved to get the best angle, and all the while Geraldine beamed.

Waiting for the journalists to settle again, I said, "Now one of my new jobs will be to help sport professionals and amateurs alike who have damaged their bodies because of their particular sport. And on that score I am giving up squash as," and here I hesitated, and then looking at Geraldine, "because," I said, "I might clank on the court". Geraldine gave a lovely giggle whilst the gathered journalists looked puzzled.

"However," I continued, "the real news is that Geraldine has a very unusual eye condition and she is gradually going blind."

The effect on the journalists could not have been greater if I had deluged the room with freezing water.

In the total silence I could feel the journalists put aside their cynical, observant, analytical views of life and emotionally embrace a vulnerable little girl who has this exceptional, and I thought, 'news worthy' smile.

I waited for a long moment before I said, "I was delayed getting here because I went with Geraldine and her aunt to Moorfield Eye Research Centre and met the specialist who has seen all Geraldine's eye condition notes.

"He feels her macular degeneration can be slowed and her condition even cured with a research programme in the USA and he is prepared to submit and then monitor her progress here in the UK.

"Unfortunately the research is costly and has to be funded for Geraldine from here. Her family have absolutely no money. The only reason she is sitting here today is because the small village where she, her mother and aunt live had a whip round and gathered enough money for the air fares. In my new role I am going to help Geraldine, if I can.

"I don't know about each of you but I feel if we can present Geraldine's case through the media outlets you represent, we can get sufficient donations to win a really important event and save Geraldine's eyesight... Will you help?"

'GOING TO WAR'

Paul stared at the reflection of his face in the computer screen. "It doesn't matter," he thought for the umpteenth time, "that three quarters of their 'Policast' liquid rubber products go to the concrete industry for casting their texturing concrete sections in the building business, the stupid technical questions I get asked that the customer should know the answer to, bore me rigid." He sighed, looking at the screen.

Here we go again; of course I understand Mr Harmsworth's points. Well he makes them every Friday morning at the sales review meeting. 'We make two thirds of our profit from the concrete fabricating companies, so let's keep them sweet however daft their questions are.'

"It's all very well for him to say that," thought Paul. "He doesn't have to explain time after time how to use the formula to calculate the weight of silicon rubber they need to use for each of their jobs, by estimating the volume of the concrete part and then using the perfectly straight forward 'Policast' ratio, which after all is provided with every delivery of the company's products, to calculate the amount of liquid rubber needed for the job."

"Oh well, here we go again. I bet it's the same 'smart arse' who came on last week asking me to confirm his calculations. It really would be easier if I went down to the site and did the calculations for him. Ok, here goes my reply, all 'sweetness and light'. "Your calculation looks spot on Earl, don't hesitate to call if you need any more help. Regards, Paul."

The phone on his desk came to life. "Paul, could you spare a minute?"

"Sure Mr Harmsworth, be right up. Now what on earth does he want? Still it's bound to be better than battling some of these stupid technical marketing questions back to some of moronic customers."

"Come in, Paul, sit yourself down. Now I wonder if you could do a little job for me. Between ourselves I should pass this little job to Fred Higgins as our shop manager, but as we know he can be a bit 'Joe Blunt', well 'Fred Blunt' at times and this job needs a bit of political – small 'p' – handling. I'm in a bit of a spot as I signed up personally with the chairman of CBB, you know the Confederation of British Business, as a member two or three years ago at one of those business lunches. I realise now we really have not had any benefits from membership and I decided we are not going to pay the £1500 sub this year, so I would be grateful if you would use that diplomatic charm of yours to phone the area branch office, here's the number, and cancel our membership. Sorry to ask Paul."

"No probs, Mr Harmsworth, I have left Ken to catch our technical queries, and actually he is getting pretty good at dealing with issues, and if he gets bothered he has enough sense to ask," replied Paul.

"That's good to hear you are pleased with Ken's progress," said Mr Harmsworth. "Well let me know when you have connected the CBB."

Paul's call to the CBB was passed to the area organiser, a Mr Wells, whose response to Paul's message was to ask if he might visit to accept the resignation the following morning.

Mr Wells' courteous enquiry seemed reasonable and Paul agreed to the request, a little intrigued to meet the area organiser of a large national organisation, frequently on the TV or in the news on matters affecting business and industry.

That evening at the flat Paul explained his unusual job for the next day to Lynda. His partner usually had to listen to Paul's grumbles about doing the job for his customer's technicians, while they had a glass of wine together, and so the CBB project caught Lynda's interest. She was after all quite well aware of CBB's role in her own job as a marketing manager in the New Town's largest PR and Marketing Company. "Well you might find the man interesting," she remarked.

"Well, yes, I might but I am just going to close the membership for Harmsworth, so I don't expect Mr Wells is really going to give me much attention tomorrow morning."

Despite saying this, Paul was intrigued by tomorrow's events and as a result he delayed mentioning as he had intended, that next month would be the second anniversary of their living together and wouldn't it be a great time to make their togetherness, official! And no it was nothing to do with pleasing her mum, or his mum. It was something he really would like to do … as she very well knew.

Why Lynda was holding back Paul just did not know but she was. Anyway what with one thing and another and the CBB meeting with Mr Wells in the morning, Paul put his anniversary celebration thoughts on hold.

At nine-thirty precisely the receptionist called through to Paul to say a Mr Wells was in reception to see him and Paul in his rather better office suit and unusually with a tie in place, shook hands with a tall, grey-haired, distinguished Mr Wells who turned out to be Trevor after the pleasantries were over, and he and Paul were seated in the little meeting room off Policast's reception area.

"Sorry the coffee is from a machine, Trevor," explained Paul.

"Oh, this cup is excellent and going around the country I frequently have to drink some pretty dire versions with a show of enthusiasm," replied Trevor. "I hope you won't mind, Paul, but I have brought you a copy of a CBB internal report which covers the last three months activities where the confederation was able to contribute an industry business point of view which otherwise would not have been aired to the media or politicians. Of course I do realise Mr Harmsworth feels that there is little to be gained by remaining in membership, but I wonder if you might indicate one or two issues from the report which I think do cover matters of importance for your own industry before he takes his final decision!"

"Unfortunately, Trevor, the recent election results have caused several companies in our area to consider their membership with our newly empowered political group, seemingly rather more interested in supporting the unions' points of view than this country's business leaders," replied Paul.

"To my mind," said Trevor, "the very time we should be using CBB resources and experience to present a balanced view of the options."

Trevor pointed out several of the summary points in the report and Paul, who liked to keep up with the ebb and flow of business politics following the recent pre-election media cover, felt he had been able to make one or two sensible comments and Trevor seemed to respond to these with genuine interest.

"Now, Paul, I have several more meetings today and I must be on my way. I can say refreshed by your interesting view, and of course my cup of coffee. If you could give me a call when you have talked to Mr Harmsworth, whichever way he decides, I would be most appreciative."

With a full load of work to deal with Paul decided to give more time to his thoughts on why he had not, as yet, cancelled CBB membership despite his instructions to do so, before he spoke to Mr Harmsworth. In any case following his discussions with Trevor Wells, he felt decidedly unsure as to which line he should take on the whole matter.

Lynda had no such confusion when he returned to the flat that evening, after he had showed her the CBB papers. "Harmworth's making a mistake and you will have to convince him it's in the company's interests to support CBB."

Paul was stung to reply, "It's all very well you saying that but Bob Harmsworth is the owner and my boss and he is a man who decides on the strategic direction that Policast takes, and let's face it, he is pretty successful in his choice of directions."

"Nobody's arguing that," was Lynda's response, "but he clearly is not up to speed with what CBB are dealing with which, it seems to me, have some value to the company."

Still far from being sure Paul knocked on Bob Harmsworth's door soon after 8.30 a.m. the next morning. "Morning, Paul," he said, "tidied things up for me with CBB?"

Paul eased into a response which began with, "I have been looking into the value of our membership with the help of an internal information sheet Trevor Wells, the Area Administrator, went through with me."

Paul quickly found himself making a case to retain the membership which he thought as he spoke was the right thing for the company.

At the end of ten minutes of explanation, which Bob Harmsworth listened to without interruption, Paul said, "Of course, Mr Harmsworth, I can phone this morning and do as you ask, but I just felt you should have my views on the other side of the coin!!"

Bob Harmsworth was quiet for a minute or two, looking at Paul, before he said, "Okay, young Paul, we will stay in, providing you get involved with CBB as our representative."

A somewhat chastened young manager phoned Trevor Wells to explain that his boss had changed his mind but there was a catch. Trevor Wells' response was immediate and enthusiastic. "I am putting you on our County Committee. Can you come to the New Town Community Centre next Tuesday evening at 7.30 p.m.?"

The mid-sixties Community Centre for the New Town was a large drab and rather formidable complex of a film theatre, a dance hall and various ancillary meeting rooms, serviced by a less than popular restaurant made all the less inviting by the rainy evening.

After failing to find any reference as to the location of the CBB county meeting room, Paul finally found an employee who 'thought it was on the fourth floor at the end of the corridor'.

The corridor was illuminated only by emergency lights as Paul walked down to the formidable twin doors at its end.

Pushing open the door, expecting a room full of business people, Paul surveyed a long green baize table above which were a single row of lights leaving the majority of the room in semi-darkness.

Trevor Wells hastened over to Paul. "Welcome to our little committee," he said.

It subsequently transpired that thanks to the recent political changes and the sluggish business climate, the bi-monthly county meetings were very poorly attended and the CBB HQ administration was very focused upon trying to retain existing members as their first priority.

At the end of the meeting a somewhat bothered, but proud, Paul had agreed to host next month's Sussex County Luncheon meeting with heavy assurances from Trevor Wells that everything would be arranged for him. All he had to do was welcome the speaker and 'be nice' to the members who turned up.

Paul practised his welcome speech in front of the bathroom mirror and, with the help of Lynda, considered the choices of what he should wear for the occasion and felt his suit, shirt and tie would be best suited to a business men's luncheon gathering.

In the event he need not have bothered too much as the eight local businessmen from the area who had paid for lunch had turned up. Several according to Trevor after the meal had paid but failed to show blaming more pressing engagements.

Those that did turn up wore a range of styles from jeans and jersey to the 'suit and boot' standard that Paul had anticipated. None the less, as Paul explained later to Lynda, he felt his welcome to the gathering around the single table in the hotel's ante-room had gone down quite well and Trevor Wells had been effusive in his congratulations.

Paul also felt, as he related events to Lynda, that his introduction for the speaker that Trevor had arranged, an 'expert' on marketing analysis techniques, had gone down well, which was more than the speaker's dry, academic, and rather boring after lunch dissertation had done.

Two months later there was a repeat luncheon performance with a speaker on 'Health and Safety at work' and ten local business members attended, none however Paul noted from his first 'hosting' event.

Trevor arranged for a discussion in a pub on the borders of Kent and Sussex, inviting Paul and the recently appointed 'host' for the Kent CBB luncheons for that county's members.

As it turned out, Trevor was called away after a pleasant pub dinner, leaving Paul and Carl Adams to commiserate over a couple of beers.

Having exchanged backgrounds, which placed Paul and Carl in the same age group, it emerged that Carl worked in a large paper producing company, a member of the sales team. He had been deputised by the sales manager to 'look after' the company's CBB connections at more or less the same time as Paul and, despite Trevor Wells' enthusiastic support, Carl was having no better success in getting support for the bi-monthly luncheon meetings than Paul.

Football dominated the conversation as they relaxed together and the current media coverage of violence of the supporters of several of the Premier League's top teams was a matter that they chatted about.

Carl went to the bar to get his round and returned to find Paul furiously writing on the plain paper back of a bar menu. "I've got it, Carl. I know how we might get some CBB members to support the lunches. I think the two counties should go to war."

"What, go to war, what sort of plan is that?" was Carl's response, plonking two pints on the table.

"Well, look," responded Paul. "I've got the basics written down. Your lot have the Channel Tunnel across to France right! We have the Gatwick Airport. Okay, both are important trade links for business in the UK, never mind our counties! Now, my plan is, I will pass the word to our local paper through a mate I have who is one of their junior reporters, that the CBB Sussex members think your lot are not promoting or using the Channel Tunnel to develop business for the South East."

"Got it," said Carl, "and I'll tell a guy I know well in our local rag, your lot are not encouraging development of Gatwick Airport as a source of business development for the South East. A matter deeply resented by businessmen in Kent. A cracking idea, Paul. Do you think the local press will take the story up?"

"Well, it's up to us to convince our contacts. After all most of the stuff they print week in week out is pretty boring, so let's hope for the best," Paul concluded, finishing his pint.

A somewhat surprised Trevor Wells phoned Paul to say he had over forty-five luncheon seats booked for the following week's meeting. Paul explained the 'war' plot he and Carl had hatched up and a somewhat anxious Trevor said, "Oh well, let's just hope we can keep the members coming, and at least with the numbers we have for both meetings I can get a couple of 'heavy weight' speakers."

In the event Paul's luncheon went well with an interesting speaker followed by a vigorous question and answer session where the need for improving trading techniques and conditions with the EU were widely debated as was, to Paul's surprise, what could be done by CBB to improve the transport facilities through the Channel Tunnel, cut out traffic backlogs and cross-border procedures.

With the debate leaving the speaker and Trevor busy making notes and promises to respond to members as a matter of urgency, Paul had to be quite determined to close the meeting only ten minutes over the scheduled finish.

Paul phoned Carl to find how his day had gone the following week to hear that events had proceeded in much the same way, and he had some difficulty in maintaining discipline in the question and answer session following some pretty ludicrous statements about obstructive airport procedures in Sussex constraining international trade.

Both Paul and Carl agreed their little 'war' idea had at least caused some interest within the business communities.

The next meeting was a very different event. The local paper journalist had suddenly become a 'close friend' of Paul, promoted to this position by his editor, and in this condition ready to buy him a lunch pint at the drop of a hat.

A rather more scary reporter from the national press was waiting by Paul's car one evening when he left work to enquire how serious was the commercial enmity between the business communities that 'his' meeting had unearthed?

Paul did his best to explain, without divulging the real reason for the whole piece of theatre, suggesting a fierce commercial rivalry had always existed. He was, however, some way short of confident in feeling that the reporter bought into his version.

Trevor Wells phoned a week before the next luncheon meeting to say that he had booked the ballroom of the hotel as the numbers of members and their guests had swelled to one hundred and seventy-five and he was limiting the event to two hundred.

Trevor also said that the 'success' and he sounded anxious when he said this, meant that the CBB Chief Executive was joining the lunch, and they had engaged a well-known MEP to speak.

Paul arrived at the meeting venue early and was somewhat impressed, although anxious, to find the CEO of the CBB would be sitting next to him on the top table.

With the help of Lynda and much practice, Paul had carefully worked out a thirty second welcome, with references to the distinguished guests, and a comment on the importance of reasoned debate on developing commercial services within the county. He felt instinctively that it was important to keep everyone calm and the question and answer session to reasoned debate.

The lunch went well, although in his super-sensitive state Paul could not help noticing the number of jugs of beer which seemed to be flowing into the hall.

The CBB CEO had been rather complimentary about the way Paul had helped to increase the members' involvement and their interest over such a short period, although Paul wondered quite upon what their increased interest was focused.

Dessert had been served and Paul had just begun to feel everything was going to be alright when it all went very wrong.

Suddenly from the back row of tables a huge banner appeared, held up by at least half a dozen of the members' guests. Denouncing in large white letters on a green background 'Any intention to expand the Airport would be detriment to the County Environment.'

The banner was then paraded round the hall with the lead group chanting a rather repetitive slogan whose words were far from clear in the growing hubbub.

The appearance of the banner and the chanting seemed to activate a range of protest groups and the noise swelled to a roar as face to face arguments, illuminated by mobile phones flashing in all directions, turned the hall into a human maelstrom.

Paul felt he had to do something as host. He rose to the microphone as a prisoner might approach a lion in the Roman arena with a short sword, noting as he did so the national press reporter was pointing his camera in his direction, as Caesar might have done with his hand before inverting his thumb.

Paul recognised his voice was completely inaudible above the noise as members and their guests stood and shouted at each other. The whole catastrophic scene crystallised itself for Paul when a flying bread roll hit the leader of the environmentalist banner group in the eye.

Soon after this event the police arrived to separate the warring factions and create some order. Paul noted as he gave his name and address to the police inspector, that Trevor Wells and the CBB CEO had evacuated the scene and the 'battleground'.

Just before the police had arrived in force, Paul thought it must be very like any premier football match owner felt after a fracas between team supporters, as he wended his way home in disconsolation, filled with apprehension for his future. He could hardly believe how horribly out of hand everything he had done had become. Who on earth was going to take him seriously again? How on earth was he going to explain his disaster to Lynda?

Paul had the flat door key in his hand when Lynda opened it from inside. He was about to speak when Lynda cut him short with, 'Your event is being reported on local radio and Mr Harmsworth's been on the phone and wants to speak to you as soon as you get in. Could you call him please?"

"He wants to fire me I suppose for bringing the company into disrepute," was Paul's depressed response.

"I don't think so," Lynda went on, "but I have some news for you as you have become so risk taking. I have called your mother and mine this morning and told them that we are making everything legal and getting married. They were delighted."

Paul was standing at the door with his mouth open, when the phone in the hall rang, insistently.

"Hallo, Paul. Bob here. Congratulations that delightful partner of yours, Lynda, told me you had finally agreed to make her an honest woman. You did a hell of a job energising the CBB, it's all over the news. They will be well pleased with the increased membership all this publicity will create. Paul you have clearly shown how positive and forward thinking you are, just what we need now in the company. Take it easy for the rest of the week and on Monday we are going to talk about your future here at Policast. Oh and I hope you will invite me to your wedding."

"LOOKING FOR THE HIGHGROUND"

"You see," said Mr Fothergill, fiddling with the letter in front of him. "I have held this information up for a few days while I argued but really have no options. The new owners want to centralise their operations and, well you can understand, your role as operations manager on this site is… well, redundant."

My immediate thought was, "No, I don't understand and after thirty years working for your company, I resent being pushed out. I don't feel any better because I know Mr Fothergill, you will get a nice fat cheque for your 5% share of the business and you will connive to get them to want you to stay on now as their 'man'."

Mr Fothergill was twiddling his gold biro pen, a sure sign he was bothered. This anxiety reaction, I recalled, was usually a prelude to his request to me, 'Could you sort it out and let me know what you have decided.'

How many times have I done that for him? Let's face it, I have been doing his job as general manager for … what? Five years at least … and somehow he will convince the new owners he is the man to be their general manager.

Mr Fothergill slid a typed paper across his desk towards me from under the covering letter. "The CEO and the HR Director have been quite generous in their proposal for your redundancy payment," he said. "Of course, I pushed for the best figure," he added hurriedly. "Why don't you give the arrangement some thought and let your people know. I expect you will want to chat to your wife and we can talk again in a couple of days before you meet the new owner's HR management. Err," he added, "I would of course like a full brief on your, that is, the company's programmes. Perhaps it would be helpful and tidy if you could type out the details and let me have them before our discussions."

"Of course you would," I thought, "otherwise you wouldn't have any idea of what is going on... So you can convince your new boss what a clever, on the ball, fellow you are."

Without a word indicating my displeasure, I picked up the typed sheet and walked out of the office.

I walked through the small and rather crowded Operations Centre filled with three people and their desk computers and several filing cabinets. The place was unusually quiet for a usually cheerful, noisy unit.

Clearly my team had already worked out the new owners would want changes, although they certainly did not know how dramatic these would be, and although Mr Fothergill had not mentioned my team, I was sure the piece of paper in my hand would be indicating the direction the new company was keen to go.

"Alice, do you think you could fetch me a cup of tea?" Alice looked up from her computer screen. "The kettle's on, I will bring it in in a mo," she said.

"I do have a proposal paper from the new owners, via Mr Fothergill," I announced to all three of the team, now looking up from their screens. "And as soon as I have a clearer picture, I will talk the details out with you so that we can decide upon a plan."

I deliberately said "decide upon a plan", thinking as I did so, "these guys deserve my best shot, and I am not having them pushed about, whatever I am forced to accept."

Seated in my office with a cup of tea, I began looking through the several pages of the directive, noting the minimum statutory approach, defining my own redundancy package and this despite Mr Fotheringill's assertions.

I found each of my team had also been treated in the same casual, minimum statutory way. The order from on high dictated that closing of the company's operations unit would be completed a month from the redundancy notice, allowing, as the document dictated, an orderly detailed hand over of all operational programmes, projects, as well as the files for company personnel. Apparently the central administrative department would then assume responsibility for all the company's operational activities from the first of the following month.

"Well," I thought, "there it is in cold impersonal words, the abrupt and toothless end of the road in a few brief words for, what is it?"

I began to calculate my forty years and then thinking about the team: Alice, my secretary, thirty-two years in the company. John, let's see he started in accounts before he came over to operations, he is a year younger than me at fifty-nine, and he is proud of the fact he was recruited when he was eighteen, so there is another thirty-one years of real commitment; even our "legal eagle", young Gillesby, what is he now … must be… of course … his fiftieth birthday party was only last year. How could I forget that hangover! And he came to the company straight from school and went through all that day release until he became qualified. I still remember the honours award ceremony as top student of the year, so he must have been one of the team, for what, at least thirty years. So all in all that means, putting aside the clerical support team and their comings and goings, the core operations team have given, let's see, one hundred and thirty years of service, and I mean good service, to this company, and now we are out, disposed of in a couple of weeks with a cheque and a pat on the back, professional life, well mine anyway, over!!!!

I realised, as I sat gloomily reflecting on the future, whilst I would have to accept that I was never going to get a comparable job at my age, the career situation for the other members of my great little team would be difficult, if perhaps not as impossible as mine.

Forcing myself to focus on the facts, I became sure I could find a home for the three clerical staff somewhere else in the company before the "shutters" came down, but my senior team "well it's no good I have to deal with the miserable facts and share the bad news with them", I said to myself.

Alice ushered them in and it was immediately clear they were expecting bad news.

I felt a little better getting the three of them to sit at my planning table in their usual seats, as we did at the beginning of nearly every working day, as I began to explain the contents of my communication from the new owners.

I did not even bother to try to suggest Mr Fothergill had fought to get the best terms possible for us. They would have all known that would have been a fabrication of the facts. They all knew we had been propping up his executive role in the company for years and they had on many occasions seen how he took the plaudits from our owners, now ex-owners, whenever he could.

I got the points across without having to blow my nose, although it must have been clear how upset I was. I apologised that I had to explain the miserable detail, saying that I fully intended to take a properly detailed case up to the new owners' Head of Personnel. I glanced at the typed signature and title, HR Manager, Mr R A Pullman, FIPM, and then said, "Mr Pullman and I fully intend to press a case to get each of you a redundancy payment which reflects not only your years of company service but your real managerial contribution to the successful growth and the profitable performance of the company, of which you should be justifiably proud and since I am on this point I can truly say, I think you are a very creative and professional team, and I have been very proud to be a member of our team."

At this point I blew my nose vigorously, while they all looked at me.

"Well, thanks guys for taking the wretched news so well. I shall now go and arrange with Fothergill." I just decided "Mr" no longer fitted the bill. "To get the visit to the new owners over and done with and perhaps you would each help me by getting a list of the programmes?"

At this point I realised I did not have their full attention. There was a passing of paper and a couple of computer sheets and a whispered comment from Alice to Gillesby which I caught as "I think you should start" – start what I thought?

Gillesby cleared his throat and said, "We actually had the news a couple of days ago."

My mouth probably dropped open in amazement. "You knew all about the changes?"

"Well," said Gillesby, "we did, and we discussed the matter and decided you would have to go through the 'process' to ensure you could state to the new owners and that pompous idiot Fothergill that you had professionally complied with their wishes. We knew you would be upset and on our side – as we are on yours – and so if you don't mind I will explain what happened."

"I wish you would," I said, sounding as if I had a woolly sock in my mouth.

"Actually," said Gillesby, "chip in guys if you want to." He continued, "Fotheringill's secretary, Jo-Ann, you know she came back last year after the baby and had to work for him, saw the correspondence from the new owners several days ago. She became incensed that he was sitting on the instruction, taking absolutely no action, to give you the impression he was fighting for a better deal for you … and us … and she deliberately listened in as he talked on the phone to Mr Pullman, whose discussions were all centred around 'what I have managed', 'what I have created', 'how I direct', all me, me, me.

"Jo-Ann took a copy of the instructions and gave them to Alice, just saying she felt the way Mr Fothergill was behaving was disgusting and she thought we ought to know, and as soon as she could find another job she was leaving. We have put our heads together and think there are one or two things we could bring to the notice of the new owners which might strengthen our hand."

Here Gillesby paused, as the other two nodded agreement and I sat back feeling rather confused. "Well perhaps you could explain what things…!"

"Unfortunately," said John, "we learned from Jo-Ann that a meeting has been arranged for you with Mr Pullman for the day after tomorrow. Fothergill of course kept this back until you had 'surprised' us with the news. He will, we suspect, be telling you this sometime this morning. Anyway, we are working on a couple of ideas, but we think one matter you could introduce that would certainly slow the amalgamation down, would be the company's pension plan. We checked out the other five companies in which the new owners already hold the majority shareholding. They all have final salary pension programmes and we were able to get the background info on the funds, liquidity related to pay out and the individual company's legal commitments. Each scheme is significantly smaller than ours but under the new Pension Act if the new group amalgamates our final salary pension plan into their group responsibilities, as they are proposing, they would be legally liable to up their existing schemes to match our pension's financial reserves, and we calculate this would cost near enough, seven million."

"Good grief." I was flabbergasted. "My goodness guys, you really have hit on something here."

"Well," continued John, "we figure if you bring in this surprise to Mr Pullman, he will have to share the information with the new owner's CEO, who we hear is a straight speaking tough operator, who built the business up from nothing. We were hoping you would be able to use this pension situation to put a case to the CEO that we would be better left to manage our own business for him."

Later that day, Fothergill called me back into his office.

"I have arranged with Mr Pullman for you to go to a personal meeting with him to review the hand over procedure now that you have had the chance to explain to your people the changes," and he added, "given them the details of their redundancy payments. I have the details of our … err, the, programmes you sent through."

"Not," I thought, "that the detail will help you much with your lack of background knowledge."

"And," continued Fothergill, "Mr Pullman and I have spent some time discussing how the programmes can be smoothly conducted."

"I bet you have," I thought.

"He, and I, have agreed to co-operate together on all the details of the administrative items to ensure all aspects are properly covered … in the interests of course of the new owners," he concluded, rather lamely.

"I will be ready for the meeting and will do the best I can, Mr Fothergill," was all I could manage to say.

"I'm sure you will," said Fothergill, waving me in his customary way out of his office.

I arrived fifteen minutes early at the commodious reception area of our new owner's head office, embellished with numerous photos of sporting teams, presumably representing the group, several with the chairman, Frank Baggott, passing out cups and prizes.

There were several other visitors who had recorded their presence, when at five to nine precisely Frank Baggott walked into the reception area and I was pleased I had looked at the photos to recognise him as he said, courteously, to the waiting representatives a cheerful, "Good morning." The response was unanimous and he then walked through, presumably to his office.

My appointment for nine o'clock was missed as I waited for Mr R A Pullman's call, and by nine-thirty I was the only one left waiting.

At this point Frank Baggott walked back through reception and having spoken briefly to the receptionist, he came across to speak to me.

"I am sorry you have been kept waiting," he said, adding to my amazement, "Frank." He then went on, "Mr Pullman will be right along but it does give me the opportunity to welcome someone from the working team of our new acquisition."

Standing, I took the opportunity to say, "Well, thank you, sir, I'm only really here to hand over our work programmes to Mr Pullman as unfortunately I, and the operations team, are not required under the reorganisation."

At this point the internal door burst open and a flustered portly gentleman scurried across to us.

"Oh, I had not realised you were waiting. I am so sorry," he panted out. "I will certainly be catching up with you, Mr …" He tailed off, desperately trying to recall my name.

"Frank," said the chairman. "Well I am sure you will give this young man your full attention."

"Of course, sir, naturally," Mr Pullman spluttered, as the chairman went on his way.

Once settled in Mr Pullman's, not leather bound visitors' seat in front of his large leather topped desk, we got down to the detail of the programmes to transfer activities to the new owner's operational group.

It quickly became evident that Mr Pullman had no real intention of getting into the detail and frequently referred to 'matters' that Mr Fothergill will "I am sure be 'covering' next week."

After an hour of fairly fruitless discussion, I decided that it was not appropriate to raise the issue of pensions until the end of the meeting. I was just about to do so when the door opened and the chairman walked in. "Now, how is it going?" the chairman enquired.

"Oh excellent, sir", was Mr Pullman's swift reply. "We have covered all the important points in the hand over and …," he looked at his notes, "Frank has been most helpful."

"That's good," said the chairman. "Are you comfortable everything we are picking up has been covered?" he said, addressing me.

"Well, sir, there is one issue which bothers me," I replied.

"So, what is that?" asked the chairman, sitting down.

"My concern is the company's final salary pension fund," I said, whilst pulling out the file from my briefcase. "My team have been doing some work and in summary, sir, your six company acquisition funding is averaging 44% funding cover. Whereas our company is funded to a level of 58% and as you know, sir, the legal requirement once you amalgamate, my team have calculated, the group final salary pension scheme will require your company to contribute," and I addressed my computer sheets for several minutes, quite unnecessarily, "seven million, one hundred and thirty-two thousand as soon as the restructure programme is integrated."

I noted Mr Pullman had gone deathly white.

The chairman addressed him calmly, "Did you have this detail from Mr Fothergill?" he enquired.

Mr Pullman sounded as if he was being strangled.

"Oh no, sir, no, sir, not a word, sir … err, this comes as a complete surprise, sir."

The chairman looked at me. "Frank, I wonder if I could ask you to go and sit in reception for a minute, get Jessica to get you a cup of tea or coffee."

I floated out of the office, feeling I had just gained the 'high ground' in what I hoped would be better terms for my team.

Sitting with a cup of tea, my mobile rang. "It's me," said John unnecessarily. He sounded excited. "We have found another useful 'negotiator' for you," he said. "The Middle East Alcesta project, it is currently generating nearly 22% of our earnings before interest and tax."

"Well, yes?" I said.

"It seems," continued John, "Gillesby has spent most of last night going through the whole contract and he has spotted in the small print that if the principal contractor is in any way changed, the requirement is to re-negotiate the details of the contract, not close the contract, but the Arabs can insist upon a price adjustment and we know in the present climate that would be definitely down, making the new owner's purchase price of our company a good deal less attractive to their shareholders."

"You guys are brilliant and I do mean brilliant, and tell them I think I already have the 'high ground' up here. I will call you later." I responded as calmly as I could!

An imposing lady with large glasses came into reception. "I am Miss Jenkins, the chairman's secretary," she said, quite unnecessarily. "I wonder if you would mind joining the chairman in the board room." She said this in such a friendly way that I followed her cheerfully.

The rather imposing board room, with a table that could certainly seat twenty, had the chairman at the end and two suited, grey haired gentlemen seated one each side of him.

In a chair behind these three, sat Mr Pullman, I noted still looking pale and with a white handkerchief clasped in his hand, as if he had been recently perspiring.

"Thanks for coming in, Frank," said the chairman. "This is Jeremy King, our Finance Director, and Norman Wheeler, our CEO. We have had a quick look through our group pension details and your own, and it is clear you were perfectly correct and spot on with your figures. We shall therefore not be transferring the pension arrangements up here. Now, I wanted you to meet my senior team, but before anything else, is there anything else we might not have spotted, or missed?"

"Well, sir, there is one thing that could be a problem," I said looking at him and the other two directors. "My team have been carefully going through the supply contract with China."

I then explained the potential dangers of the new owners merging of administration.

The audience was most attentive, without raising any questions. The chairman looked to Jeremy and Norman. "Perhaps I could leave you to chat over this problem with Pullman? Frank, I think you deserve a lunch, would you care to join me?"

In the chauffeur driven car, the chairman said, "Jeremy, Norman and I have been rethinking things, thanks to facts you have brought to our notice." We will be leaving the operation issues with your company and we hope that you, and your team, will consider joining us. We will, of course, honour the redundancy payments and if you, and the team can accept the new employment terms, which I can promise you are rather more favourable than your existing arrangements, you will be reporting to Norman and splitting your time between the units. Oh, and should you be wondering we have already moved Pullman to a new role, and we will be offering Fothergill a statutory redundancy package."

Later in the day I texted Alice and asked her to get the team into my office. When I called them I started by saying, "I am standing on a hill and have a beautiful view to share with you."

MARKETING FLEXIBILITY

"It will never work," said Rosemary in a slightly stage whisper to Ruth and Rachel seated to her left and right in the back row of the canteen, where the 'R3' team of receptionist/telephonists could observe the majority of the haircuts, hairstyles and backsides of the entire company of twenty seated on the singularly uncomfortable chairs in the canteen, the banner hung over the serving hatch proclaiming 'Home of the Spotlight Recruitment Agency'. One of Gerald Mason-Brown's, the CEO, little motivational ideas!

The staff were all unusually still and attentive, waiting for the CEO, who had just cleared his throat for attention and was about to hold court, in his double-breasted suit, twirling his heavy horn rimmed glasses in his hand to give further emphasis to his impending announcement.

Rosemary – Rosie to most – was very sensitive to the moods of GM-B, experienced as she was over several years by taking his mail to his office every morning and responding to his "Morning Rosie, what trouble have you brought this morning?" by giving him a run-down gathered from her half-hour of close investigation of the envelopes as she had her morning cup of tea in the post room.

Tax, finance demands, finance services, enquiries about job opportunities, clients' responses to interview offers, supplementary information from clients, companies' requests for recruitment information, panics from media outlets for personnel complaints. Rosie had an unnerving feel for the content of a letter simply by holding the envelope in her hand for a moment or two, and considering its weight and origins. On the occasion when a personal letter arrived for GM-B, she had also been especially helpful by suggesting his lady friend of the moment might tone down her use of perfume when sending her little notes to him. Just in case the formidable lady wife of GM-B dropped in on her way to a Bridge Day or ladies golf tournament!

Normally Rosie would settle GM-B down by passing to him each rubber-banded individual pack of envelopes with a yellow sticker, indicating any significant content under her carefully handwritten note along with her comments on current issues for the agency.

"Light on the interviewing responses this morning GM-B. Quite a return from that local newspaper ad last Friday," Rosie commented.

GM-B never allowed his secretary to open the envelopes until he had been through Rosie's morning procedure. Probably, thought Rosie, because of the 'revolving' nature of GM-B's secretaries, who were generally newly out of the secretarial college and whilst generally were of the age and looks which impressed those coming to the office to be interviewed for a media job, they rarely stayed long enough for the aspiring candidate ushered into GM-B's presence by the same girl for their final interview.

It was widely acknowledged by the company, down to the office junior, that Rosie had the 'ear of the CEO' and it was wise to go along with her whenever possible, and certainly not get on to her 'black list', otherwise you would find that as the R3s were at the hub of all communication, the chances of progress within the company were slim indeed.

Ruth, who liked to record everything and anything, had her iPad at the ready as GM-B warmed to his theme.

"We here at Spotlight Recruitment are very conscious of working at the cutting edge of technology to ensure we maintain our leading role within the media world." GM-B was very fond of using the latest buzz words when addressing an audience and none more so than today, sensitive that he was making a 'historic' statement for the company.

"We," he said, eyeing his top table of directors. Harold Staplehurst – Finance, Nick Spode – HR, and the newly arrived member, J.J. Hicks – Marketing, pausing long enough to make clear that he had full support of the board for this auspicious statement. "Have asked J.J. to carry out a full survey of our marketing position in the month he has been with us."

"Typical," thought Rosie, "making sure if things go pear shaped he has someone to blame."

"And," continued GM-B, "we are today announcing the implementation of a new marketing strategy which will keep Spotlight Recruitment at the forefront of media recruitment."

GM-B smiled confidently at this point before putting on his heavy rimmed glassed to read from his notes.

"In a week's time, we are switching from our present 'office residential mode' to a 'flexible working mode' whereby you may all choose your daily place of work. We are calling this 'Free Range Working'." As he continued, GM-B smiled one of his 'confidence' smiles to comfort any who were anxious about the news.

Ruth, typing notes, muttered, "Free range chicken, more like!"

GM-B swelled on. "With J.J's experience we are committing ourselves to a trial period from next Monday during which you can personally choose to work from home, or from your favourite café, or should you wish to find a seat and a desk anywhere in the company premises where you feel comfortable working, and can change your venue as often as you feel you wish to. Now, I shall be working from home and using my office for ... um ... administrative reasons from time to time, and so I would be grateful if nobody chose my seat to work from for the moment." He guffawed loudly at this point without getting much of a response from his audience.

GM-B adopted a serious and confidential tone as he continued. "We will make careful preparations over the next few days to prepare each of you for this new flexi-working approach but you are, of course, all well equipped with the latest smartphones, laptops and access to superfast broadband so like Google and Facebook, this company can fully benefit from a flexible work place mode that the board know will encourage the best performance possible from you, the talented and creative people that you are, as we expand our search for individuals to fill recruitment vacancies for our media and film company clients."

GM-B took a sip of water from the glass at his side and continued in the same serious tone. "Just as important to me, that is to say you, as you offer your time and skills to people out there in the market who are looking for an agency to help them find a step forward in their career, or a new film or media role, J.J. has calculated that our new 'Flexible Workplace Mode' will offer us the opportunity for a 30% growth phase over the next twelve months. I repeat a 30% gain and I can see from your expressions you are busy calculating what benefits this will have for your personal bonus scheme. Quite right, quite right," repeated GM-B. "That is the attitude we want."

"Now, what we have to do, of course, within our 'Free Range Working' arrangement is to maintain a strong communication link for all our team to the centre here and to keep a close eye on any 'step forward' contract or programme. J.J. and Harold have devised a straightforward electronic linkage conduit system that will allow you wherever you have chosen to work on that day, to centrally communicate so that, where necessary, the full force of our resources and support will be at your disposal as you work with your client in the café or in the garden at your home, or wherever you choose to work."

"Now I know," said GM-B in a fatherly way, "this news is a lot to take in at this point but as you know with one or two of our competitors crowding us, particularly over our biggest film contract to date with Global Films, the board felt it would be better to announce the changes as quickly as possible so that you can have detailed discussion groups with your sections in preparation for next week. Now, one final administrative point, our admirable reception/telephonist group, led so well by Rosemary." GM-B smiled towards Rosie on the back row. "The three R's will be the hub of our communication network within the 'Free Range Working' structure."

"First I've heard of it," said Rosie irritably to her two colleagues as GM-B closed the meeting.

A little time later, seated in their office behind the reception desk, Rosie said, "I think GM-B's out of his depth and he has panicked because he is hearing from Global Films that if we don't come up with more placements suitable for their technical support team for their international blockbuster '009 Dreadlocks', and do it quickly, they will pass the contract to those dreadful people at WeFind4U Agency. I know," continued Rosie to her compatriots, "that Harold is dead worried that if we cannot fulfil the contract this year, we will go into the red and in trouble with the bank, which is why GM-B panicked and brought in – at a high salary I am sure – that J.J, impressed, no doubt, by his 'just out of business school new marketing technology' and he has given him a free hand to bring in this stupid 'flexible workplace' rubbish. Well, girls, we have to see if we can help GM-B through this crisis!'

Rosie got up from her chair and walked round the office to stretch her legs before she continued. "Those three lads who are supposed to be digging up candidates in this field for us, are they the ones most likely to give us a lead on what's happening out of the office? Ruth, Terry is the leader of the pack and he has always fancied you. Get him to explain how he would like to keep in communication during this trial period, and, oh," to general laughter, "it will not be necessary – whatever he says   to visit his pad. The farthest you can go is the Broadway Café which is, I suspect, where we're going to find most of the company working anyway!"

"Rachel, could you buttonhole Harold and gather as much info as you can on the money issues. He's desperate for a friend to talk to, so I'm sure if you keep him supplied with coffee and biscuits he will give you lots of detail about what's going on, money wise!"

"Meanwhile, I will see if I can find out what makes J.J. tick, or at least try to work out how much he really understands about the scheme he has sold to GM-B. We will have a review of events once I have gone through the morning's post from tomorrow onwards."

"Okay," said Rosie to her girls the following Monday, "let's summarise."

"Rachel, you have the feeling that Harold feels the company is sliding down the slippery slope to bankruptcy unless we can sign up at least fifty technical support people for Global Films this month … to date we seem to have only four likely placements. Ruth, you are going to see Terry and his two side-kicks at the café on Wednesday, if by then he has got any info on potential candidates or actually signed anyone up we will have some guide as to how events are going to unfold."

"In the meantime, girls, gather views and opinions as we go, from everyone. As I said," Rosie continued, "I have drawn a blank on J.J., he clearly has decided to avoid me like the plague and seems to be travelling all over the country and for all I know, stopping at bus queues to ask if there is a film techy waiting for a bus he can give a lift to! GM-B has told me to call him at home on his mobile if I am worried about anything in the mail and give all the financial stuff to Harold. I will give him a week working from home before he is back in the office. Otherwise I'm just going to open anything I am worried about and pass it on to anyone I think can deal with it … A fine state of affairs really."

The morning post room meeting on the first Friday of the new procedure was a very sombre affair.

Rosie looked at the neat pile of envelopes awaiting GM-B's return.

Rachel had just passed the information that she felt Harold was heading for a nervous breakdown, trying to deal with the financial pressures. Not helped by his ladies' team coming and going in the office, most giving priority time to their small children's school arrangements and understandably taking the advantages of 'Free Range Working' with home management now as their first priority.

Ruth's report from her regular visits to the Broadway Café to catch up with Terry and the sales boys, although punctuated by the "do you know how much I have spent on lattes and those chocolate cakes, it's scary", was beginning to establish a clear picture that the boys were having no success finding media techy specialists in the café, or any of the other venues they had frequented, and they were heartily fed up with J.J. constantly 'dropping in' to check on progress.

"It wasn't as if," Ruth explained, "he ever put his hand in his pocket to get them a coffee."

Finally Rosie said, "This whole silly project is killing the company." She said this whilst holding an envelope embossed with the showy gold logo of Global Films in her hand. "GM-B has said open anything I am worried about, and I am worried about this letter," she said, slitting the envelope.

Ruth and Rachel sat anxiously with interest as Rosie scanned the single sheet of paper. Finally, she said, "They have fired us." She went on to read the contents of the letter.

'According to the Director of Administration our people have become aware that your people are frequenting coffee bars, cafes and clubs trying to attract technical support staff for the blockbuster project '009 Dreadlocks', a procedure which is not in line with Global Films thinking, and further since Spotlight Agency has, despite the initial claims, failed to achieve any of their target recruitment objectives, we regret', wrote the Director of Administration 'that we are terminating our contract forthwith. Yours faithfully ...,' Rosie finally intoned.

Ruth was looking horrified. "Does this mean I am going to be out of a job?"

"Not necessarily," said Rosie, "but it is now up to us to help GM-B. Ruth go down to the Broadway and get Terry and his two side-kicks and bring them back, right now. Don't tell them or anyone about this letter."

"Rachel," Rosie continued. "Keep away from Harold and say nothing about the letter. I'm not going to tell GM-B, he would be in here panicking with all sorts of silly directions if I did."

Later, sitting with Terry and his two assistants, the 3Rs had 'discovered' some chocolate biscuits and with a wide choice of tea or coffee "Free" as Rosie explained to Terry and the boys, she explained the purpose of the meeting.

"This discussion must not go outside this room – all agreed? Ok," she said, "we are going to have to save this company. I don't think J.J. has any idea how to manage his scheme. Harold is in a panic of his own. Nick has his head in the sand and GM-B is desperately hoping the scheme is going to work, while he tries to keep out of his wife's way at home. I bet he is doing a shop in the supermarket as we speak! Now, before I tell the board we have lost the Global Film contract and we all start looking for another job, has anything happened which might give us an opportunity to keep this creaking company afloat?"

"Well," Terry said, "me and the boys were talking in the pub last night and we listed the number of 'flexible contract' people this new Government scheme is encouraging to get short term work, you know without a contract or commitment to the number of hours they can work."

Ruth chipped in. "Yep, my brother's doing his Uni and any spare hours he is up the Victoria Hospital getting paid for a few hours there as his degree work allows and he was telling us there are masses of people at Uni who could do flexible paid hours work if they had a bit more time to investigate the flexible work opportunities that are available."

The discussions flowed freely for some time as tea and biscuits disappeared.

"Ok," said Rosie, "let's agree we don't say anything to anyone. We will all try to gather info on organisations, companies etc. who will take on individuals for short term working under this Government scheme. Wherever we can we will get together a list of students or anyone ... yes, including mothers with young kids who could do paid work for a few hours in a week given the opportunity. We meet again on Monday."

There was a buzz with the tea and biscuits in the post room where the six members of the team reviewed their progress, without Rosie giving the post any attention at all.

Looking through her notes Rosie said, "We have eight organisations, the Victoria Hospital, two supermarkets, the Central Car Cleaning Company, three garden centres and the Broadway Café, all ready to pay us a weekly retainer if we can send potential flexi-working hours candidates to them, and you have already found forty-seven students, pensioners, people between jobs, ready to sign up to us if we can help them get a few paid hours work every week. Ruth has all the detail but the sooner we propose this new 'flexible contract scheme' to GM-B, Harold and Nick the better. I think I will tell GM-B there is a letter he has to see tomorrow and I expect he will be in like a shot … we will then give them the picture."

"By the way, Terry, J.J. called in to find where you were and I told him you were working on a big case and you were expecting to make progress over the next couple of days. He said he would come in to the office then." She gave him a conspiratorial smile.

Later on Rosie reported, "The meeting went beautifully to plan. I did not spare GM-B – the silly ass – the pain of reading the letter from Global Films. He practically expired. Then Terry and I laid out the new 'flexi-contract scheme' and he had Harold and Nick in the office working on the details in a flash. Incidentally," continued Rosie to the two girls. "Terry was promoted to Marketing Manager on the spot, about three minutes after GM-B had phoned J.J. to tell him his scheme had flopped and caused the loss of the company's largest customer and he was therefore no longer required."

"Weirdly," said Rosie, helping herself to another éclair, "just after the meeting Terry took a call from the CEO of 'WeFind4U'. He had heard we had a new department who could provide short-term workers for general and administrative jobs under a 'flexible contract' and his company had been overwhelmed with demands for technicians which they were having a great deal of difficulty finding, and so they had all their regular staff out looking. Could we help to cover the administrative gaps in his company? Terry thought we could…"

MY TERRITORY

"John, we will of course give you the fifty year badge at your farewell dinner and as you know HR are starting your company pension payments from the day you leave. We cannot have a valuable employee like you missing out."

'Ironic,' John thought, 'since it seems that it was my suggestions to the board that have resulted in my losing my job!'

John was sitting in front of the chairman's desk with a cup of tea in a fine bone china cup and saucer, with a digestive biscuit on a matching plate.

'Even more ironic,' thought John perched on his chair, 'since the last time the chairman had declared his 'value' to the company was years before when he had arrived on the shop floor with a crowd of shareholders, and several financial journalists, giving a tour of the plant and, by all accounts, a significant lunch at the local hotel where copious amounts of fine wine flowed, all the shop floor gossip had it, to ensure maximum favourable column inches in the business press.'

John could count the number of times the chairman and he had talked on one hand, since that fleeting tour which had been rushed rapidly past John's office, until the last two weeks when John's little office booth again seemed to be the focus of changes, positioned as it was in the middle of the main production line. It had, for years, given John the best view of the manufacturing facility from his elderly leather padded rotating chair. A view John needed in order to spot any hitch or glitch with a man, or a machine, that might disrupt the finely balanced flow of manufacturing activity, essential to the carefully planned sequence of activities his efforts and skills had brought to the shop floor.

Now thanks to the overzealous interference by a trade union representative, John's view had been constrained unless he took the effort to raise himself three inches off his seat to peer over the white plastic frieze that the shop stewards, and a couple of his left-wing cronies, had insisted upon to stop John, as they said, 'prying' on the hundred or so shop floor employees, who were being 'unnerved' by his scrutiny, which in their lengthy protest claim to the HR manager, could easily cause an employee to have an accident on a lathe or a drill. A clear breach of Health & Safety rules, as they explained to the HR manager, who would do anything to achieve a quiet life and who went along with the demand, despite John's assertions at the one-sided meeting, that maintaining the flow of work and ensuring its smooth progress was a function of his own role, and also a safety feature of importance.

As a result of the meeting a white plastic strip was inserted on to the three sides of his booth, so John's receding hair line could just about be spotted from outside the booth.

John did consider, for a moment, having four three inch wooden blocks made to raise his seat to the level that would allow his customary vision, and then decided the inevitable wrangling would not be supported by management.

As it turned out, John soon found there were good side effects from having the barrier in his booth!

The first advantage arrived with his mug of tea from the canteen the very day after the maintenance crew had put up the screens.

Mabel, the rather nice girl from the canteen, who brought in the tea (one of the few perks of his role) and usually slipped in and out with no more than a shy smile of acknowledgement to John's, "Good morning Mabel, how are you today?" or sometimes to vary the one way exchange. "Let's hope we have a bit of sun this weekend." Or other minor pleasantries which only ever enlisted a slight smile and a nod of the head, before she departed back to the canteen.

On this the first morning after the 'remodelling' of his office, Mabel put the tea as usual on his Union Jack cup mat, and then sat down in the office chair at the end of the table loaded down as it was with tool sets, drill pieces and other bits and pieces needed for the assembly floor.

John was, to say the least, surprised at this turn of events. More so, when Mabel said, looking round, "Much better, it was time you had some privacy".

This aspect had not crossed John's mind, but it did at that point and he agreed. "Yes, I have been looking for some privacy for some time, it's like living in a goldfish bowl", John concluded, pleased with himself.

In practice, much to John's surprise, employees on the line seemed much more confident to talk to him in the 'renovated' office and share matters which they certainly had not been privy to in the old open environment.

In the strangest of ways, the new privacy also seemed to bring the senior company management into closer touch with his opinions, feeling free to discuss the options they might be considering for schedule changes, or new product introduction, John decided, free from the tool setters who were dab hands at lip reading as they gave the impression of setting up machinery in proximity to the booth.

The following week John brought into the office one or two personal books on photography, his hobby and passion. After eating his customary sandwich, a lunch prepared each day by his wife Jane with, as always, a piece of fruit, John felt comfortable reading a couple of chapters of the latest book on photographic techniques free from prying and, no doubt, judgemental eyes.

A less attractive change but just as surprising a few days after the 'remodelling' event, the door opened and the chairman stepped in and sat himself down in the spare seat.

John was shaken and very nearly suggested to the chairman that he put a newspaper down on the seat for fear of getting oil on the rather silky blue mohair suit. Then he thought, 'what the hell, it's taken him years to sit on the seat, why should I care?'

"John," the chairman said in a rather familiar way, "the board are making a few changes and with your experience of laying out the manufacturing sequences so successfully, we would like your opinion of one or two proposals we think would help growth."

John felt flattered by the invitation and accepted the report the chairman passed to him, and agreed to get one of the typists to type out his comments and let the chairman have them in 'a few days.' With this and a cheery nod, the chairman left.

Within the hour the company general manager, like John a long term employee and a man determined to keep out of any potentially controversial activity if he could possibly do so, dropped into the office.

"John, this reorganisation thing the board are all on about", said the general manager. "Careful what you say, I'm sure they are looking to reduce costs."

John thought 'and I bet you are on the list', it being generally thought by the company supervisors, that the general manager spent his time crunching numbers and manipulating schedules and had no more knowledge of engineering or production processes than the company's medical officer.

Having decided that the general manager's 'careful comments' might well be designed to safeguard the existing process rather than properly consider any significant changes, John gave over the whole evening to consider his response to the report.

John could see the value in several of the board's suggested changes. Other changes being driven by the strategic operations the board considered were necessary in entering new markets, he felt he would be exceeding his role on which to comment. So, having considered at length, John passed his report to a typist the following morning as the chairman had requested.

'That', reflected John, balancing his bone china cup and saucer, 'is why I am in the chairman's office getting thrown out of the company early.'

The chairman explained that John's comments had gone down well with the board. The only negative factor had been, it seemed, the reorganisation would no longer need a production planning manager, and John was therefore no longer required several months before his formal retirement date. The chairman felt sure John would understand, particularly as the company were honouring all his pension commitments!

The retirement dinner went well and nice things were said before the 'keep in touch' handshakes.

The long planned trip to Australia went well and although both John and Jane found the experience exhausting, were not unhappy to leave their Australian cousins and their family, or leave the jogging, swimming, fitness lifestyle which seemed to dominate life and the Aussie sports events, success and failures which seemed to dominate conversation for much of the time.

All things being equal, it was with some relief that John arrived home and started to consider how he was going to fill his days.

After two or three weeks of thinking and spending time at the library perusing photographic literature and meetings at the local photographic group, a period when several friends had made various suggestions about taking up cycling, joining a golf club, on and on, despite the fact that John had always known from his school days, he was uncoordinated, if not cack-handed as he was never picked for any of the school sports teams although, he reflected, he was an active member of the Flora & Fauna Club!

After a time John recognised, looking at himself in the shaving mirror, he was feeling 'flat'. Well, 'down'. He might even be feeling 'depressed'.

Matters came to a head a few days later. John was weeding the virtually perfect rose bed under the sitting room window that was open to the spring sunshine, when he heard voices from the visiting group of women from the Ladies' Circle taking their customary tea and scone visit with Jane, who was talking and said "It really has become so difficult. John is constantly under my feet nowadays."

The words struck John like a hammer blow. 'What,' he thought, 'has happened to my life and what is there left for me to hope for?'

John went to see the family doctor the next day and explained, "I have lost the discipline of my life, going to work every day, meeting my colleagues, keeping my job going. Suddenly I find myself with more time on my hands than I know what to do with. It was all so unexpected and now I am upsetting Jane's routines and if this goes on we are going to fall out."

"To be honest, Dr Jefferies," continued John with a strained voice, "I seem to be irritable all the time now and it's getting worse and it really isn't very long ago that I was 'thrown out' of the company, early, so I'm just thinking I'm going to be in a real mess in the future if you cannot help me sort my new life out."

"John," said Dr Jefferies. "You have made yourself very clear and that is the first step towards recovery. I've looked at the few tests we've done for you today and I can see no problems for a man of your age, except perhaps the increase in blood pressure we have recorded today over your last few years' performance. So, if you are in agreement, I would like to talk to Jane on the phone as the other member of the team, before I prepare a little plan for you or suggest a course of drugs."

A week later John was back in Dr Jefferies' surgery. "John, I do have a few steps to help you but before I do I would like you to agree to take a short trip which I think will help take down your blood pressure to a safer level after the jump up again this week."

"As you are no doubt aware," continued Dr Jefferies, "the National Photographic Show and Exhibition is in Birmingham and my brother-in-law is a keen enthusiast, like you. Here is his mobile number and he knows all about your photographic equipment and technique interests. As he lives in Perry Barr close by the exhibition centre, he has arranged for a good bed and breakfast for one night next week so he can meet you and take you to the exhibition for a couple of days. I'm quite sure you and he will get along well with your common interests. I really think this sort of break will help bring that dangerous blood pressure level down and then I can start you on your course of drugs to help the depression. I also have a suitable analyst in mind to give you some psychological help over this difficult period."

Jane had clearly been given the background and need for Dr Jefferies' plans to reduce John's blood pressure and had already packed an overnight bag by the time John returned home.

The exhibition was as interesting as John knew it would be and Dr Jefferies' brother-in-law was a knowledgeable and entertaining guide and companion over the two days.

Despite the enjoyment and the piles of literature John had collected, the clouds of darkness were gathering in his head as he took the train south and his lonely feeling of depression was setting in again as he paid off the taxi cab at the gate to his house.

As John trudged to the front door and felt for his key, the weight of the future seemed to weigh on his shoulders.

The door opened before he could insert his key and the noise from the house shocked him into open mouthed amazement.

The normal peace and tranquillity of No. 11 was replaced by noisy chatter, and loud laughter. "Come in dear," said Jane. "I do hope you enjoyed your trip. Oh, there are several of your colleagues here to see you." She ushered him into the sitting room where John found ten of his old workmates seated or standing everywhere in the room.

As John stood in the doorway, amazed, the welcome reached a crescendo. Finally John's old general manager said, "John, we have a bit of a surprise for you, well it was Mabel's idea", and everyone smiled in Mabel's direction as she sat demurely on the sofa.

The general manager continued with a warm smile, "We all felt that the board took advantage of your skills and experience, letting you go without recognising your value and contribution, and we felt we might be able to do something about it when we heard from Jane how difficult you had found you're first few weeks out of the company".

John continued standing, still amazed, looking at the HR manager nodding, senior charge hands, setters he had worked with for years, all taking tea in his sitting room.

Mabel stood up. "Come on, John, we have something to show you."

Taking John's arm, she walked out of the sitting room, down the corridor into the kitchen, with everyone crowding behind, through the back door and into the garden.

John staggered, and was held on either arm by his old colleagues, as the group moved towards – sitting squarely in his garden on the side lawn – HIS OFFICE. Solid and square, the windows on three sides, partly covered by the white screening.

Mabel marched to the metal door and it swung open and John was pushed to the front and over the step into his old office. It's leather seat, table, shelves, cupboard all there and gleaming.

John could not take it in. He was dumped unceremoniously down into his old seat and it was only then that he became aware that his camera equipment and books were all resting placed on his shelves.

"We decided with Jane and Mabel's help, you need your own 'territory' and as the board had mistakenly decided your office, or you, were not needed in the reorganisation," explained the general manager, "I commandeered the office before it was destroyed. The maintenance team fixed it and moved it to your garden so you have a place of your own."

"Now, I have a surprise for everyone, including you John," the general manager continued. "I have here a letter from the chairman which I will read to you, if I may." With that he opened the envelope and read out, 'Dear John, I hope you have settled into your new lifestyle but I wonder if you would consider giving the company a few hours of your time every month as our 'Consultant Advisor'. The production assembly arrangements within some of the strategic changes have not developed in the way the board envisaged. I have asked the company HR manager to prepare an offer to allow you to consider the consultancy role, and I and the board would be most grateful for your assistance in this matter.'

The HR manager then produced a fat envelope from his top pocket and with a smile handed it to John.

Everyone smiled and sitting in his old seat in his 'Territory', John smiled.

NEW VENTURE?

As I swung into the car park at the back of the bank, I could not suppress the feeling of anxiety, even dread, welling up inside me.

How has everything I worked for come to this? Could I, should I, have managed things differently? Why did I not see the disaster coming? After all, the cards were on the table and had been for ages, years probably.

If I hadn't been so... confident! So sure everything would go on just like before, I might have avoided today, but who could I, should I, have turned to. Nobody in this 'criminal crowd' waiting to dump on me in the bank today!

They're all sitting there with their smart suits, with their wives out playing golf together, waiting to dictate my little company's collapse just so they can get hold of my site for their fancy, high price, property building programme, that everyone in the village is dead against.

All the villagers' meetings and appeals to the planning authorities to stop this crowd developing their high cost homes programme got nowhere and really hasn't helped me at all now the local planners are on my back about the building.

The 'criminal crowd' don't live in the village and they certainly don't care that five hundred expensive houses, sold out to commuters going to London to work every day, is going to wreck a village community which has survived supporting each other for centuries and is still ticking over around the pub and the local shop.

"Oh, it's no good, I will have to go and face the music," I mused, as I straightened my best tie in the car rear mirror, thinking as I did so, "how many times have I thought that with, what is it? 108,000 miles on the clock, I really should change her – if I could afford to do so, which I can't."

No point taking my file of papers into the meeting. They know all about my business. "Why did I sign away the freehold of the site to cover my overdraft at the wretched bank?" I pondered, knowing they had already decided my future whether I liked it or not.

"Do come in," gushed the bank manager. "You know everyone, John Cook and Cyril Hardy from Global Developments? Please sit down where you are. I am sorry that we are having our little get together in the bank but as we have all been through the proposition on paper – well several times, I do hope you won't mind us meeting like this so we can get things going?" All this said with a fixed half smile on his rather florid face. The same unpleasant half smile I remembered when he told me that 'Head Office' had told him to close my overdraft facility, based I recalled, upon the lack of profitable performance over several years.

I noticed the nods of approval from the developers sitting to his left and right.

"No, of course not," I said, thinking, "the slimy fool knows I have a week left to pay off my outstanding mortgage, and he already knows I have no chance of selling off enough of my stock, despite all my efforts, to cover the repayment demands."

"And," I thought, looking at the two young developers in their sharp, grey, shiny suits, both sipping water and shuffling papers, "everyone here knows I am in a forced sale, with the site being valued to cover my bank debt, with scarcely any money being added for the company stock valued at scrap levels."

The whole charade focused upon getting me out and the buildings flattened in preparation for the house building programme.

A lifetime's work building up my component distribution gone, with my signature on the paper now being slid across the table towards me by Cyril Hardy with a "If you'd care to use my pen" offering his heavy gold pen to me as he did so adding, just to rub salt into the wound, "If you have time to join us for a little celebratory lunch afterwards, that would be fine."

I looked at the agreement in front of me, still upside down, and suddenly the resolve that I still did not know I had, stiffened within me and I thought, "I still have a week so I cannot just give in and give up."

"Gentlemen", I said, standing up amazed at myself as I said, "thank you but I am still investigating options and have three days to do so, and so if you do not mind I will look through your documents with my advisers and get back to you before the end of the week."

"What adviser?" I thought as I looked at the row of faces opposite, cheered by the various looks of surprise and disbelief on their faces as I swept rather theatrically out of the bank office.

"Well now they're going to be really pissed," I thought as I climbed into the old Ford and pulled my tie off, "and I am not going to get any help over the timescale for clearing the stock off the site once they start clearing the site", as I had imagined I might have been able to agree before I went to the bank office and as I had thought, to sign the agreement!

Back at the company I walked through the little sales department where everyone was 'heads down' at their desks or 'eyes' fixed on their computer screens.

Everyone expects me to make a 'we are closing the company' speech today crossed my mind as I let myself into my office and looked at the pile of unopened correspondence on the desk in front of my seat.

I had hardly started to slit the envelopes before the door opened and Betty, one of the two typists we have on the payroll, who acted as an occasional secretary, came into my office. "A man from the Planning Health & Safety Department is waiting to see you," and having glanced at a visitor's card, she said quietly, "A Mr Giles. Shall I make tea?"

"Okay, show him in," I replied. Although the thought of having to deal with a planning official at this time when I badly needed to think, knowing the old structure was not in good shape by current standards, or rules and requisitions, filled me with a feeling of depression quite extinguishing the sense of regained confidence following my surprising stand at the bank meeting.

Mr Giles entered the office and as I rose to shake his hand, I had time to reflect that his well lived-in grey suit and similarly rather careworn briefcase matched his rather tired smile as I offered him the chair opposite my own.

"I hope my secretary," I hesitated momentarily as Betty did not always come across as the 'secretary' type – indeed as she made comments such as "I'm looking after him" that she liked to tell all and sundry, often in a way which was specific to her East End upbringing, I was however very aware of her genuine care and concern particularly through the last months of struggle with the bank and finance.

Mr Giles took his coat off, laid it over the arm of the chair and carefully placed his briefcase neatly by his side, and sitting down extracted a thick file of papers, all I noticed in an unusually careful and precise manner.

Rather than let him open the almost certainly difficult discussion, I suggested he might like to await the arrival of the tea. Mr Giles looked up from his papers and smiled an agreement.

I opened the conversation by expressing my own 'difficult start to the day' without being specific but concluding that this was a week I could 'do without'.

To my surprise this elicited a response in the same vein. "My week has also been disappointing," he said. "It will be the last week in my job after forty-nine years with the council. In fact," he continued, "you will be my very last job."

At this point it was very clear to me he was quite emotionally upset, if carefully controlled, and I responded with what I hoped was seen by him as real concern, saying, "You must be at the point of contractual retirement?"

"Oh no, not really. The new management have put aside the old procedures where I could have continued to use my experience, which is everything in this role, in the interests of cost cutting." And despite his careful and calm presentation of his work situation, it was easy to see the bitterness this had caused.

Fortunately Betty burst through the door at this point with our rather battered tin tray, our large teapot, two mugs, despite the fact we had a set of perfectly good china cups and saucers for visiting customers, together with a plate of scones and strawberry jam, that her mother provides and are the same that take the prize for scones every year at the local Ladies' Guild cake competition.

Mr Giles and I both relaxed as Betty mothered us with the tea, scones, jam and cream, to the point that Mr Giles became 'Sam' and addressed me comfortably now on a Christian name basis. Perhaps because we were both being stressed by life outside our control, or wishes, the discussions became more intimate.

"I don't know if you are aware," said Sam, "but when I did my survey of all your buildings a month ago I found the biggest Building 'B' was of a most interesting construction."

"Well," I replied, "I didn't realise there was anything special about 'B' other than it is the largest building we have and it rather limits my ability to extend any of my other warehouse units."

As we were talking freely I was then able to explain that "Warehouse 'B' was the first unit on the site put up by my late father, who had started the family component distribution company. Firstly, distributing car parts, electrical and otherwise and he had extended into supplying classic car components.

"When he had become ill, expecting to recover, he had asked me to leave that side of the business alone until he was well again. I had agreed, locking building 'B' up so, as he put it, no one could muddle his component stocks and details.

"Unfortunately my dad never recovered and I had left the building locked up as he asked, and to be honest I had my hands full with my then growing electrical component distribution business."

"Well that explains quite a lot," said Sam. "Your dad must have had the building made to limit any fire hazards as the walls and roof are lined with asbestos because of the special components he was keeping to distribute to classic car renovators, and classic vehicle rebuilders. What I suspect you also are not aware of is, your dad had collected a useful – perhaps valuable – collection of at least a couple of classic cars in parts, crated in your Unit 'B'."

I leaned forward in my chair and said, "Good lord, I had no idea. Well now that I think back I can remember an old car body and wondered why he would bother to give the thing space – a long torpedo shape – I suppose it had two seats at one time many years ago."

"Well you are right," said Sam, "that car body is a 19...... and I suspect from a cursory look at the crates around it, the complete car is in your Unit 'B' waiting to be rebuilt."

"Wow, I'm sure that has some value, and thank you as I really had no idea. I had wrongly imagined that the whole place was full of fairly useless motor bits and pieces that I would have to unload for a price once I have sold off all my electrical and electronic component stock. Although with immediate pressure from the bank on my overdraft, I am not sure I have time to do anything."

"Being honest with you," I continued, "my position right now is I have to pay off my overdraft by the end of the week and I am under all sorts of pressures to sign away the whole site so that the developers can get on with building the first batch of one hundred town house units, and the bank can clear off my overdraft."

I realised I sounded more and more despondent as I intoned the facts of my position, so I added "Look, I am very sorry I am burdening you with this, you have got your job to do."

Sam was sitting silently whilst I shared the misery, looking intently at me. He then said, "Look, can we agree to talk absolutely confidentially together?"

Without any hesitation I replied, "Absolutely."

"Well," said Sam. "My wife passed on a couple of years ago and we had no family, so apart from my car 'Violet', I am rather concerned that I have never been a member of any club or group. To be honest, apart from listening to classical music, I really don't have any hobbies. Which, I now realise, will be a problem at my age having been," here he hesitated, "well, thrown out of my job with the council, despite the fact that I have years of real experience with hazardous materials, and substances, in buildings, factories etc. and I have been the only one dealing with these matters within this area of responsibility for the council. Responsibilities, which incidentally, are not going to be covered by the joint Building Maintenance Team that has been set up to centrally cover all the council responsibilities, including Health & Safety within buildings. I think I can rightly say, I am something of an expert on asbestos control and safe disposal." He stopped. "I hope I am not going on too much?"

"Certainly not, just a minute," and I banged the top of the brass plunger bell on my desk. Betty shot in as if I was being assaulted by someone. "Betty, I wonder if you could rustle up a pot of tea for Mr Giles and me." She recognised that I was not being threatened by our council official and did not need to come to my assistance and disappeared to find the company's 'Visitor Tea Pot'.

"Please go on, Sam," I said, "you are beginning to give me the impression you might have a plan which perhaps could help my miserable position, or am I being too optimistic?"

"Actually I do have a thought or two which might help me, as well as you. That is if you don't mind me presuming a little about you're … eh … difficult situation?"

"I don't mind in the slightest. To be frank, Sam, I am down to the wire over how I might save my business and I really have no idea how I can hold off the blood sucking developers who I am sure are hand in hand with the bank."

"Well," said Sam, "I'm certain I can hold them back for a bit. That might give you time to find a way out of the problem".

"Any idea, anything, I am all ears," I said beginning to feel some excitement at the prospect of a solution.

Sam looked at me and said, "I suggest I slap a Case D27/14/M1 form on you as current owner of building 'B'."

"Err, yes, right, what exactly is a Case D27/14 or whatever you said notice?" I mumbled.

"Well, when I place the enforcing notice on you as the owner, it means a material investigation must by law take place, using the National Building and Materials Evaluation Centre and no work can be undertaken until that evaluation of the building cladding, interior in your case, has been completed. Including, of course, the demolition of the building, until the officials clear either the acceptability of the asbestos lining or declare the material in a dangerous condition requiring an expert company to remove the asbestos and clear the roof and walls before any demolition can take place."

"I am," continued Sam, "quite sure the lining is in excellent and safe condition, indeed normally I would give you clearance but in the circumstances I suggest I place and record the D27/14/M1 conditions on the building."

"Ok, but what happens then?" I queried. "What happens then? I mean how will it help?"

"Well," he replied, "when I record the legal obligation back in the office, the procedure is in place for a visit by an official from the evaluation centre. He is a good friend of mine, Charlie, we have worked together for years. I can tell you now, he will find the building fit for use but with their present workload this form will not get to the top of the file for, say, five or six months at the best. Now if I may suggest, I give you two copies of the legal demand for you to give one to the bank because if they foreclose this weekend, as I understand your comments, the bank assume ownership of the building as part of the process of recovering your overdraft debt."

"I suggest," he continued, "they will immediately recognise the potential cost liability that would be their problem and they will back away from forcing you out of ownership."

I am now looking at Sam as if he is a visiting witchdoctor who has given me a potion for eternal life.

"And," continued Sam, "if you give the second copy to your developer friends, they will recognise their carefully calculated costs and timescale is in jeopardy and they will back away and, I suggest, back down on their offer to purchase the site."

"Sam, you are a genius. I am overwhelmed by your idea ... uplifted ... to be honest reborn.... if you know what I mean!" I blurted out and continued. "Listening to you I wonder if I could suggest an idea, that I hope you will see as helpful to you. Would you join me as a partner next week when you are free of the council and help me sort out my dad's collection of classic car components so we can dispose of the lot in a tidy way to a dealer to get what we can, and I am more than prepared to share whatever value there is with you if you could sort out and list the bits and pieces. Whilst I see what I can do to dispose of some, or all, of the electrical stock, thanks to the time you have so marvellously found for me?"

"Of course I will," said Sam. "I will be here first thing Monday and I am delighted that I can look forward to an activity for next week when all I could think about when I arrived here was a black and blank future stretching from Monday onwards. I am going to complete the D27 forms, leave you two copies and whistle back to the office to undertake my last task by recording the form on the register, which means whether I am there or not, the legal obligation is in place. Now time is short so I will get going, and I think you will be busy delivering your notes. I look forward to seeing you on Monday."

This said, Sam got out an official looking form pad and began to write as I collected the tray and tea things to almost waltz into Betty's office, which called for her to explain loudly, "Good gracious, what's happened. You won the pools?"

Opening my post in the office ten days later, I was really waiting for the morning arrival of Sam from his new workplace in Building 'B'.

The door opened to introduce a new style Sam, resplendent in pale blue overalls and a yellow baseball cap with a Ferrari badge predominant above the peak.

"Morning, Sam, you are looking extremely sharp this morning," I said smiling at him. And he was, and I assumed the smile he had on his face was down to the fact that he clearly loved his new job sorting and referencing the huge number of classic car components in boxes and crates left by my father, a job that would he assured me, take several months.

Pleased as I was to have Sam as a rather different partner, the letter I had just opened brought me down to earth with a severe bump. "Oh hell," I said to Sam. "You'd better sit down, this is a real stinker," and I read out to him, "it's from Knight, Plank and Frottage, who are apparently lawyers for the bank."

Scanning the letter I told Sam, "It seems they are taking me to court in three days to recover the overdraft without waiting for the findings of the materials investigation centre which," I said to Sam, "means I will be declared bankrupt and will not be able to trade next week."

I rested my head in my hands, elbows on the desk. "Honestly, Sam, I just don't know how to keep going."

"Leave it to me," said Sam, "I was just coming in to give you a bit of news. When I got to the back of the central bay in 'B' unit, I found some body panels and a radiator with some crates marked ..... One of the crates had an engine in it. So last night I got on the Web and found a list of classic car renovators, thinking we must have some components they might be interested to buy once I have sorted out what's what over there."

"Well, anyway this morning I called the company dealing with classic .... and explained what I had found.

I spoke to the owner who was very excited, so much so that he is on his way down to us right now. He said to me on the phone, as an indication, if we have the body panels, the engine and the components for rebuild, and I am sure we do, he will offer immediately seven hundred and fifty thousand pounds and bring a bankers draft down, and a contract to provide us with a percentage commission when his people have completed the rebuild. These............are fetching better than two million in auction. It seems to me the bankers draft will more than pay off your overdraft and I can get on and work out what else we have hidden away."

I banged the bell. Betty bolted through the door but before she could launch her supportive tirade, I said, "Get everyone together in my office, then go to the brown filing cabinet and look on top behind that big bundle of tax returns. You will find two bottles of Champagne hidden away. I put them there waiting for my dear old dad to come back and get the business going – well, I think he has just come back!"

REFLECTIONS ON MY LIFE

I shut the car door and as always noticed the satisfying clunk click as I stared through the windscreen, driven with rain reflecting back my face in the darkness of the near empty car park.

I saw the tired grey-faced specialist again in the reflection and watched him rotate his heavy framed glasses, as with arms on his leather topped desk he said, "I am sorry to say."

I wondered sitting there now, how often he, the oncologist, had to say "I am sorry to say" and although I had accepted the "sorry" such a short time ago I now wondered if he really could be. After all when there is nothing more that could be done to halt the ravages of the cancer cells in the body, perhaps "go and prepare" would have been a more helpful comment.

A car passed the entrance to the car park and its bright lights reflected back from the water running down the windscreen, shutting out the yellow high pole lights flickering across the empty car spaces.

The momentary change of reflection made me think on what I had to do.

My mind cut back to my decisions only a few months ago where not sharing the clinical investigation with my wife, or my son, had seemed to be the positive way forward.

Not sharing the medical investigation with anyone, work colleagues, or friends, had at the time I had first felt the uncomfortable pain seemed the way to go to maintain my position and lifestyle.

My reflection came into focus again, wondering what I should do now to explain. Indeed, should I explain? After all, I mused, I had played to my "leadership", tough successful independent businessman image, so carefully built up and nurtured over, what, twenty years of developing the business, my marriage, the arrival of the boy. Indeed, the whole structure of my life. "Rely upon me", "I deal with the problems", "I direct the way forward", "Shape the strategy", "Score the goals", "Relax, accept my lead and all will be well".

How is my decline and disappearance going to be seen? When do I announce the "end game"!?

I mused on in the flickering darkness of the car. Will anyone care – really care? My son will – but will he!!!?

I saw my face again in changing detail in the driving rain across the screen – how much time this year – last year, have I spent with my wife, my son? I struggled to recall a single occasion when I had taken the boy to any important event at school, remembering painfully the recent football cup match argument with my wife and a tearful boy when I had to change the plan for Saturday's match to visit New York for a clients' meeting – "It just has to be done for the business," I explained and now remembered with shame. The "Banana Club" evenings – nights and the "business" meeting that could have been conducted so easily over the phone.

Will the boy actually even notice if I am not around?

Thoughts choked my mind with negative reminders. My wife will probably get remarried – why not, she has always liked that chap who runs the design centre where she works – what's his name – divorced last year? What am I thinking – why not, what have I ever done to support her?

Money, what emotional value does that have? Business events – I must have presented her like a business resource, good looking for her age, always smart and clearly liked by my customers, both men and women – a real business asset and used, I realised, so often to help me grow the property business!

Would I be missed at the Golf Club? I suppose my donation and sponsorship of the "Try Harder" club tournament would be missed. I bet that arrogant club secretary will miss me bringing clients for a round and lunch, but would anyone notice if I was not about – probably not?

Friends, do I have any? I have moved up and away. I cannot remember when I last saw any of my school or university friends, called them or, come to that, they have called me.

When my old school friend came over and saw the new home, when was it ten years ago? What was it he said, "What have you bought to live in, a hotel?" I don't suppose I have spoken to him since, and I don't reckon any of my old school mates would bother or notice when I am not about. Other than, I suppose, reading the occasion as a newspaper article about when I chair the local Confederation of Trade branch, or reports from one of many business trips that I push into the local papers using my advertising "with you" muscle, and I suppose some people will read my obituary!

Boy, I need a drink! I have got to have a plan before I get home!

The car purred into life and I pulled out of the car park and headed in the direction of the house, considering as I did where I might stop off to get a drink and a little time to sort out a plan to explain to my wife.

Easing through the village in the teaming rain, I saw the "Haywaggon" pub sign hanging above the narrow road and having never, to my knowledge, been to this pub I turned sharply into the pub's car park through a high wooden arch, and found a sizable, but empty, car park behind.

Dropping my Burberry raincoat over my head, I hurried to the back of the pub and pushed through the dark oak door named "Saloon Bar".

A long bar in a long room with tables to the right and a cast iron log fire at the end greeted me. The room was lit by an array of ceiling lights with plastic shades, the majority of which were not on!

I moved along the bar until I saw a brass bell with a mechanical plunger on top and a small sign which demanded "press me for service". I did so and several minutes later a door slammed somewhere and a small intense and care worn lady appeared through a curtained entrance between the back shelves along the bar, and raised an enquiring eyebrow without saying a word.

"I wonder, could I have," I began. She cut across me. "We're not serving food tonight," she said.

"Oh that's fine, I would just like a whisky." She inclined her head without looking at a row of bottles on the shelf to her left. In the gloom I saw a malt whisky with a recognisable brand while indicating a twenty year old vintage.

"Might I have a large Glendowie?" I said. She reached upwards for the bottle, still keeping her eye on me, before twice filling the measuring glass into a large glass tumbler.

"I suppose you want ice?" she said, looking at my suit and tie, now that I had removed my Burberry. "Oh no thank you, just a little water on the side please."

She pushed the glass towards me, indicating with an inclination of her head a water jug half way down the bar. "£8.50," she claimed without further comment and the tenner disappeared across the counter.

Before I completed the "please keep the change" she announced, looking at the cast iron fire in what I had thought to be an empty room. "Mr Surveyor," and disappeared back through the curtain.

Looking about, I moved to the centre of the long bar and poured a splash of water into the whisky before moving towards the seat nook to the side of the struggling log fire. It was only then that I noticed there was already a figure sitting in the shadow, presumably the 'Mr Surveyor'!

"Good evening," I said, "what a miserable night." "Evening," he responded. "I see you cut your malt?" Somewhat taken aback I said, "Well yes, I always cut my malt."

"You must have learned that in Scotland," he said. Rather presumptuously I thought.

"Well yes, I did as a matter of fact in Glasgow when I was in the military."

His interrogation continued. "Well actually I was doing my National Service in the RAF."

"Hmm, I bet you were down Sockihall Street when you picked up that trick."

"Well yes, that name does ring a bell," I replied.

"More bars per quarter mile than any other street in the UK," he said. "Beats me why people down South haven't wised up to getting the flavour out of the malt, with a dash of water, and insist on losing it by putting in ice. A stupid American idea!"

This said, he suddenly stood up and I realised how tall he was. "You can sit here, there's plenty of room." Sitting down I realised you could survey the whole bar and room without being seen.

"Is this your regular seat?" I hesitated, thinking why was I interested? I had other things on my mind than chatting to a complete stranger.

He laughed, a deep and, I thought, very confident sound. "I come here regularly and people know this is where I sit." He laughed easily again.

I felt awkward but had to ask. "Must be difficult to talk too many of your friends when you are in this little snug?"

He leaned towards me and for the first time I saw his face in the subdued lights from above the bar. It was a strong, intelligent face and instinctively I knew this was a guy who had lived and worked in many places.

He held his position and said, "I don't come here to talk to people. I don't have friends around here."

Feeling awkward again, I said, "Look if you want a bit of peace and quiet, I can easily shift over there." I waved towards the central bar area.

"Nope," he said, "this is an important day for me in my job, so if you're comfortable, sit tight."

Then without further comment he picked up my empty glass with his own and went once to the bar end, lifted the hinged section and went behind the bar to the row of upturned bottles, returning with two half-filled tumblers and a water jug on a round tin tray.

I pulled my wallet out. "Look, allow me to get these," I said.

"Forget it, they're on the house." I began to wonder what his job was!

As he went behind the bar, I realized how tall and athletic he was. He clearly had not spent his time to middle age, as I had, slouched in an overfilled office chair in front of a computer screen, or spent his time at innumerable lunch, dinner or cocktail parties following his line of work.

Seated again, he eyed me objectively. "What brings you to this backwater on such a miserable night?"

The question jarred me back to the reality of my situation of … and here I had to struggle with my memory of but two hours ago … which seemed somehow like a lifetime ago.

Clearly the lengthy pause interested him and his gaze was firmly on my face. "Well, to be honest," I said, "chance brought me here," and then added awkwardly, "I had a rather difficult meeting this evening."

Having blundered this out I half waited for a follow up question. None arrived. Just the calm gaze and adjusting my own gaze to look directly at him, I realized he could have been slightly smiling at my obvious discomfort.

Perhaps it was the whisky beginning to cast its warming spell upon me but suddenly my need to share my situation became a dominant feeling. For a moment I struggled with my basic instincts, not needing anyone's support, just instructing, before I found myself saying to this complete stranger.

"Well, I have just had some … difficult news from my specialist, which is certain to make a difference to my …," I nearly said life, but held back on that.

There was a pause while he looked at me. "Well, you are obviously a successful guy," he said, eyeing my suit and expensive tie and dwelling on my Brightling watch and heavy gold strap.

I reflected that only yesterday I would have liked the complement and responded to it. Now I felt a severe embarrassment. "Well not really, I guess I have been lucky in some ways, business, anyway!"

He took a pull at his whisky, without adjusting his steady gaze from my face.

"You want to talk about it – the doctor?" he asked in his calm way. To my uncomfortable surprise I found myself saying, "Well, if you have the time?"

"All the time in the world," he said. "Go ahead."

A cacophony of thoughts and emotions almost overwhelmed my senses. I did not know this guy, not even his name. Nothing about him. He could be anyone!!

I had no thought out plan to explain my position to my wife and family, let alone to a complete stranger. But at the same instant I knew none of this mattered. I trusted this calm, stable, strong man who somehow was not judgemental and honest. I just knew I could talk to him.

"I, I did nothing about some aches and pains, blood etc. for several months. I thought things would pass, I was just too busy. Maybe I was scared of finding out the truth and having finally had the tests, the specialist told me...," I said, glancing at my watch, what only three hours ago? "I have got three months, maybe less – there is nothing anyone can do."

I paused, feeling pleased and somehow relieved I had got it out and did not feel the worse for telling someone.

There was an almost companionable pause, while he continued his steady gaze. "A bad deal," he said in his calm way. "I guess you have some explaining to do from here in."

"Yes, I do and to be honest I don't have a plan." Saying it out loud made the problem even starker.

"Well," he said. "If you want a view?" He paused and quite instinctively I nodded. "Well," he said, "I guess the wife comes first."

"Yes," I agreed, "but just to explain confidentially. I have been such a driven idiot with my company over the last twenty years, I suddenly realise I am not sure anyone, even my wife, will really care."

Whilst he digested this unpleasant view, I thought "confidentially", what am I saying, I don't know this guy, or what he does, and here I am blabbing out the most intimate details ... I'm the guy who manages everything for everyone around!

"Look," I said. "I really do appreciate your interest, your concern and goodness knows I need someone outside my family and colleagues to whom I can talk, but just in order to give me a bit of balance, could you give me some background on why you are here?"

"Sure," he said. "I was wondering when you would ask."

"I am an independent property adviser working for the owners of this pub property. It's been going downhill as a pub for some years, not paying the rent, rates properly etc. and it's been up for sale for a couple of years. No real interest and I have been asked to sort the mess out and move things on."

"I have been handling commercial properties for some years, I guess rather successfully, but this project, this pub, is different! And to be honest it's kind of got to me. Which is why I am staying up the road and spending time here to work out what is the best way to handle things."

My professional instinct prods me to say, "Well, I suppose in a central village location, in a good area, one of the supermarket chains would see the opportunity for a mini unit, given planning." And I said, looking across the bar area, "and space!"

"You're quite right," he responded, "but somehow I just feel it's not the right option for a building which was here four hundred years serving the local community. An odd feeling for me, as I handle, what, twenty commercial property sales, many quite difficult, over a year, around the country without any concern."

"I see," I said. Knowing I did not. "This old building has got to you?"

"I guess so," he said.

"Well I really am not sure how to explain to my wife. We live rather different lives. She is an interior designer. I have been so tied up in building my property company – I can say, successfully, and you know my connections and my image in the county, I haven't had time for her, or my son for that matter … and now I am concerned … no, I am fearful and scared that she might see the news as a sort of well, relief," I tailed off, looking into the gloom of the semi-lit bar.

"You know," he said. "I remember something I read years ago along the lines of *'Fear is really a little death. Failure is not as bad as we think it will be'.* I think you just have to take the first step and give your wife the news. Separating what you are going to say before you get home, into the facts that you were given by the specialist, and the emotions as you see them which are likely to be triggered by the situation. So that your wife can see you really mean to "manage" whatever time you have left in a different way."

I started to speak but he held his hand up. "I have to go now but I will be here tomorrow evening about the same time. I will possibly be here for a couple more days whilst I decide about this project. So you know where to find me if you wish to do so." With that he stood and slid his heavy coat across his shoulders like a cloak, and extended his hand as I also stood up. We shook hands without further comment and he smiled and turned away and walked the length of the bar and into the shadow of the exit door and disappeared from my view.

I did not know what to think, as I struggled into my coat and followed his route along the bar, searching in the dark for the heavy iron door handle and letting myself out into the teeming rain.

I kept thinking of how to get the facts of my condition across to my wife when I get home. However difficult, that seemed straightforward.

First, the specialist news. Then, "You and the boy will be alright financially and you can go on living in the house as long as you want."

These seemed to be the important facts to get across, but the emotions. Well, I just could not get my mind around what these might be. At least I simply could not think how I might discuss any of these issues tonight, or come to that, in the foreseeable future.

The automatic garage door lifted and lights came on revealing my space next to my wife's pale yellow Mercedes. A most unsuitable colour but she had dug her heels in and insisted upon purchasing it. That irritated me whenever I saw it, even tonight!

I walked through the side door into the kitchen, dropping my wet coat off at the door as I went.

My wife was not in the bright, chrome and white kitchen area, as she usually was when the garage door opening announced my return, and I suddenly remembered my son was stopping over for the night at the home of one of my wife's friends. This arrangement could be, I thought, a benefit in the circumstances.

"Hello," I called as I walked through the hall, trying to concentrate upon my opening statement.

The polished mahogany double door entrance to the lounge was open and the log fire in the sculptured stone surrounded fireplace that rather dominated the large room, radiated heat and comfort.

I sank into my deep leather chair, glancing at the evening papers laid out neatly, as always, on my side table.

"Hello," I called again rather louder to hear a response from upstairs, which sounded as if my wife was on the phone. Minutes later my wife entered the drawing room.

Still focused upon my opening remarks, I was struck by the fact that she was wearing a smart suit and silk scarf as if she was going shopping in London. I cleared my throat. "Could you sit down for a minute," I said, preparing myself.

"Unfortunately, no," she replied. "I have an important meeting and I should have left half an hour ago, but you are later than you said you would be." This said rather accusingly, I thought. "And now I really have to rush."

"Before I go, I must tell you I am leaving you. I want a divorce. I have had enough of our sterile relationship and I am going to make a new start before it's too late. I know my going will not make any difference to your lifestyle, and you can easily use the housekeeper I have lined up to keep you going comfortably until you make any other arrangements you like."

"The lad knows about my decision which is why he is away for a few days and I will be staying with him at my friend's until we have sorted out our arrangements. I am sure he will want to keep in touch but he is at an age when he will have to make his own decisions."

"Of course, I have engaged a lawyer but we can talk over the detail in the next few days, but I need some space right now and I doubt this change will be any real surprise to you. After all I have been expressing my concerns for months."

"Your supper is in the warmer and I will call you tomorrow and you, or that dreadful secretary of yours, can tell me when you can spare the time to talk over the detailed arrangements."

And with this she turned on her high heels and was gone.

I sat there immobilised, frozen, unable to move or to think, except to hear the words throbbing in my head "these are the facts", "these are the facts".

I hardly slept, perhaps an hour or two, constantly worrying that I had completely missed, or ignored, my wife's lonely frustration, and growing dislike of our marriage arrangements. Even, I suppose, hate for my lack of attention in everything, except my self-interest.

To my surprise I found myself thinking, she is right to go for a divorce, and if I could find a way of continuing to communicate with her and our son, it might even be the best way to "manage" my remaining time.,

I looked at the meticulous chart I had been maintaining day by day and the pill file by the side of the bed, which the specialist suggested I took on as a member of a research programme that, as he put it, "may help to promote a better understanding and therefore solution of the condition." Well, I need not bother any more with that.

I cannot say how I got through the next day but I did, knowing that I had to keep the "facts" to myself and try to work out what to do next. Also knowing I badly needed to talk to the man in the pub, like seeing a rock in a stormy sea.

I did however call my accountant into my office and to his surprise, although he asked no questions, told him I wanted a rough estimate of the value of all the properties we own a.s.a.p.

"Oh," I said, "and you will need to engage our surveyor. Just tell him to get on with it and send in the bill."

The accountant's mouth did not actually drop open but I imagine he told the office that I had just fallen of my rocker!

The day dragged and I went back to the pub at least a couple of hours before the previous night's meeting.

Leaving my car in the large empty car park and instinctively looking around at the back of the pub, I realised how much building there was and beyond the car park a ten acre field stretched to the tree line.

Back in the bar, no doubt encouraged by a dry, if not sunny evening, the lights were on and a barmaid was chatting amiably to two pint drinking locals at the bar.

The fire was burning cheerfully and I was relieved to see the niche seats by the side were empty, although that caused me to think anxiously, "What if he doesn't come tonight? Indeed, what if he doesn't come again? How will I find him? What am I thinking, how can I possibly rely on this guy to help me? Think more clearly about my remaining time! Well, who the hell is there who I can turn to?"

I ordered a large malt and stopped the girl dropping an ice cube into the glass, before I settled into the seat by the open door cast iron fire.

Sitting there, my mind going round and round between my wife, my son, the company, and how relevant was my Will, my mind focus suddenly turned inwards upon itself. A sharp tingling sensation filled my back and down my legs, dominating all my senses. Was I collapsing under the pressure?

I stared at my hand holding the untouched whisky glass. What was happening to me? Then the sensation disappeared as quickly as it arrived.

I looked up from staring at my hand in an attempt to find stability after the sensory surge had almost overwhelmed me, to find the stranger sitting opposite me as he had the night before.

"I just had the weirdest experience," I said, and tried to explain the sensation while he watched my face with his careful gaze.

"Well," he said, "my guess would be you've had a hormone surge they call *"fight or flight"* brought on by stress and part of yours, and everyone else's DNA, from the time when your earliest ancestors had to react immediately to events in order to survive. You're fortunate you can react in this way, it will help you deal with the stress you are under."

He then said conversationally, "I have decided to hold off the sale to developers of this place." And he waved his glass towards the now quite busy bar area. "I feel something will come up, never make a decision when you are unsure." He smiled at me as he said this.

"My wife has left me," I blurted out. His expression did not change and he took a shot of his whisky.

"Before or after you told her?" he said.

"I never got the chance to explain. She told me she wanted a divorce and was packed and ready to go and left before I had a chance to tell her."

"Do you know where she is?" he said.

"Well yes, sort of, with my son at a friend's," I replied.

"What are you thinking of doing?" he asked.

"I have no idea," I said, "but I suppose she and the boy should be told about the situation."

"When you are not sure, do nothing" he said.

It seemed appropriate to change the subject but not before I had bought us both a malt whisky.

"Do you mind telling me how your sale programme for the site is going because I have had a look around outside and got my people to look into the building as an investment?" I hesitated, anxious to give some professional balance to what must seem to be an emotional interest.

"Well, I was thinking that getting the pub into a viable financial state by adding a lunch and dinner dining area with a new kitchen, would offer a centre for the village and the area." I added, "As it used to be and as it must have seemed obvious, helping me with a couple of issues."

"Well," he said, "I think £350K would be sufficient for the owners to pass over the property without them going to the time and cost of waiting for a developer to go through the planning route and come in with a bigger offer."

He stood up. "Got to go," he said, swallowing his drink, "why don't you let me know tomorrow." And gripping my hand in his steady way, smiled and left with a wave of his hand to the barmaid as he walked the length of the bar and disappeared.

I was in early, very early, in the office to the surprise of all the staff as they came in. As soon as the accountant arrived, exactly at nine o'clock, I went to his office.

"I want to buy the Haywaggon Pub and site in the village. I can pick it up for £350K and I expect we will need another £150K to develop the site."

He looked a little surprised. "It might take planning time to get agreement to build houses in that location, you know what the planners are like, and from memory that is a pretty old building. The investment money is no problem if you think the project fits your business strategy!"

"I don't think it fits my strategic thinking and I don't want to build affordable or high value houses there. I want to get the pub running again," I replied.

He stared at me in complete surprise. "Is this ... Err! Are we changing the company's investment direction?" he asked.

"No, not really. This is just a special, one off project I want to get into," I explained.

"But," he protested, "making money with pub properties is notoriously difficult in this market, and to be honest I don't think," and here he coughed, "we have a great deal of experience."

"None at all," I agreed, "but I have several other reasons for tackling this project. I will explain in a day or two. In the meantime I am going to commit to the purchase later on tonight. On a "just note down" please, I want my wife to be written into the project details as the development director for the pub and new dining facilities, kitchen etc... Okay?"

"Well, sir, whatever you want. I will push on getting the funds ready and the documents drawn up." With that I left his office, quietly.

Back in my office, I called in my secretary. She looked at me carefully. "Are you feeling okay? Can I get you anything, you are looking a little pale?"

"Thank you, I am fine, just a little tired. Do you happen to know the football club for whom my son plays? Of course, I remember, it's the Barchester Community Team. Do you think you could get the chairman on the phone? I seem to remember he is the manager of that big hardware store in Barchester."

"The "Best Help" shop," she said. "Do you want to talk to him now?"

"Yes please, if you could," I replied.

She gave me another long look as she went through the door. Clearly my decision about the pub had filtered through the office and now this unusual request was causing her, and no doubt everyone else, concern.

"Mr Balham," said my secretary as she put him through to my office phone.

"Good morning, sir." Mr Balham's approach was couched in professional tones, ready for any request for his store's wide range of home help and building services.

"Could I talk to you for a few minutes about your boys' football team?" I enquired.

There was a brief silence. "Of course," he said. "One of these days when you are less busy perhaps you could come to a home match? Your son is one of our stars now."

"Yes, I am really sorry I have missed out, but I have a programme that I thought you might be interested in." I could hear an intake of breath.

"I seem to remember reading in the local press, you are having pitch problems with the council?" I continued.

"We certainly are," he replied and went on to elaborate. "They are proposing to increase the pitch and changing facilities charges considerably and we simply do not have the funds. I have a meeting tomorrow night with the committee and several parents to see if there is any way out of the problem."

"Well perhaps I can help here. I am acquiring the Haywaggon Pub and building and as part of the package I will get the field behind which extends on from the car park. Now looking at the ground which is flat and well drained, I would have thought with a little work there would be room for at least three pitches. Would that interest you for the club?" I could feel his interest developing.

"Well I would certainly think so, although it would depend obviously on the rental you have in mind, and I don't recall any changing facility beyond the pub!" He replied with a questioning tone!

"There aren't any," I replied. "So here's the deal. A peppercorn rental, say £10, for the season. I will convert the nearest pub building to the field into a changing and shower unit as part of restructuring the rear of the site. It will take three months. You and your support team put up posts etc. and mow the pitches in readiness for taking over the ground as soon as you can. How do you feel the committee would respond to the suggestion?"

I could tell he was overwhelmed. "I don't know how we can thank you enough. The committee will be absolutely thrilled. We have been so exercised trying to keep the three boys teams going. I cannot thank you enough."

"Just give me a call after your committee meeting. I am going to push on with our project. Talk to you later." I hung up.

Impatient for the pub meeting in the evening, I used the day to progress building contractors and the legal department to prepare the documents to cover the purchase and conversion of the site, conscious but not concerned, that this unconventional negotiation might not be realised, and yet feeling confident it would be.

Arriving a little early, I was surprised to see my new found friend already in his seat and with an overnight bag next to him.

"In a bit of a rush," he said. "I have to take on a new project in Manchester tomorrow on a big commercial development. The owners of the pub here have accepted your offer," he said smiling at me, "and are well pleased you are going to maintain the site for its proper role in the community. Your people have been in touch and everything should be tidy and transferred by the end of the week. Got to push on. Anyway I think you said you have to pop in to see your specialist this evening at the clinic, and if I may say so, all this project effort seems to have perked you up and you are a lot less pale than when we first met."

He then gave me a card with a mobile number hand written on it under the title 'a passing friend'. "Call me anytime and remember the first step is the difficult one." And before I could reply, he picked up his bag and was gone.

My emotions were completely confused between an odd sadness that I would not be seeing this man who somehow changed my perspective in the last months of my life, and made me address the important things that I could still influence that might leave "markers" behind which my wife, or I suppose ex-wife, my son and colleagues, if not friends, might at some point reflect upon as having value and actions not having been driven by my self-interest.

I arrived early in the poorly lit clinic car park to pick up a batch of pain killing pills and to be told the results of my routine blood test. Not that there seemed to be much point in maintaining this activity now that the full extent of the cancer spread had been identified.

The specialist was again sitting at his spacious leather topped desk, with his heavy framed glasses perched rather awkwardly on the bridge of his nose.

He motioned me to sit on the seat in front of him and in the circumstances I felt irritated that he could not at least afford me the courtesy of his full attention to help plan the next couple of months.

I cleared my throat and said, "I am sorry, Doctor, but I did not bring in the daily trial form as after the session last week" – was it only a week ago? "I just could not bring myself to keep the trials and all those condition notes going every day. Sorry, I should have called to explain."

He looked at me over the buff report form. "Well," he said, "you may want to reconsider as your latest blood test is showing, a well – how can I put it – a surprising result...!"

TEAM SUPPORT

Ann looked at the five steps up to the yellow front door in the Victorian four-storey house, conscious that she was standing with her left shoe on the first step and her right hand on the curved iron handrail. Frozen with anxiety she saw the handrail went all the way up to the front door, past the neat sign which proclaimed 'Wellsbury Centre – All are welcome. Please ring the doorbell'.

Ann read the sign. Thinking once again, that Dr Gilesby would never have suggested she visit the centre or given her the introductory letter, if he hadn't thought it important to help her. She fingered the letter in her pocket, telling herself, if Dr Gilesby believed that talking to the people in the Drop-in Cancer Support Centre would support and help, I should try it. Then gripping the rail more firmly taking the next step upwards she told herself, "If I don't like the people I just go home. Come on girl, you can do it," and urging herself upward climbed the remaining steps and rang the doorbell.

Almost immediately a smiling middle-aged lady opened the door, with a, "Hallo, come in out of the draft, the wind does whip up this little road doesn't it. Now, if you don't mind, could you sign your name in our guest book, it's one of those Health & Safety rules, you know!!" Ann signed her name and the time, noting there were a dozen names before hers.

"My name is … Oh sorry," said the lady with a beaming smile. "I'm supposed to have my volunteer's badge on show at all times, Jessie is so insistent, but my badge keeps getting hidden behind my scarf." With her 'Pamela, Volunteer' badge was now exposed she said, rather unnecessarily, "I'm Pamela, it's so nice to meet you, Ann," having glanced down at the signing-in book. "Now, can I get you a cup of tea or coffee while you meet Jessie who is the organiser here?"

Ann found herself ushered into a large drawing room-like space that stretched from the front of the house to the back where she could see into a small back garden through the half open door.

The several sofas around the room and under the bow window were all filled with people in earnest conversation, most enjoying tea and scones, buns or biscuits, giving Ann the impression that a social tea party was underway.

Standing by the alcove which housed the kettle, cups, saucers, mugs, glasses and a range of biscuits, cakes and cheese straws, Ann felt as if she had come into a tea party uninvited and firmly gripped her handbag in front of her, thinking as she did so, she was glad she had not brought her big fake Gucci handbag that was stuffed with her makeup, things for the boys, painkillers, and that wretched stuff John had to take three times a day.

Pamela turned around from her tea making activities, offering Ann a mug of tea, her volunteer badge once again obscured. "Sorry about the mug, all our cups and saucers are out," and she waved at the seating area. "Jessie is waiting for you in her little office, through that door and on the left." And with a beaming smile Pamela left to answer the insistent ringing of the front door bell.

Ann moved cautiously to the door and through the comparative quiet of the administrative office and what looked to her like one or two individual meeting rooms beyond, she found herself looking down at a large, well-rounded lady in a well-rounded leather seat, sitting at a table covered in papers beaming up at her. "Ann, how nice to meet you, please sit down, I have had a long talk to Alexander Gilesby about you. Such a nice man and so concerned about you. You really do have a lot to deal with just now, as well as trying to keep your job in the travel agent's." All this was said in one breath with somehow managing an encouraging smile at the same time.

Ann sat on the edge of her chair, holding on to her mug of tea and her handbag firmly and stared at the lady behind the desk.

Jessie perched a pair of heavy framed glasses on the end of her, not inconsiderable, nose. "Now Ann I will just take a couple of details. I hope you will be able to visit us here whenever you can find half an hour in your busy life, and we can always pick up details as we go along. Don't let your tea get cold, dear. Now I have you living at No.3 Merton Gardens, is that right?"

Ann nodded. Jessie continued, "That's very convenient because the No.12 bus could drop you right at the end of our little crescent."

Ann explained she drove regularly into town to the travel agency where she worked, now down to three days a week because of her family sickness but she had to drop and pick up the boys from school every day.

"Lots of our clients manage to fit us into their lives," said Jessie, "when they face stressful times for one reason or another. Now you do know we make no charge for any of our services?" Ann nodded. "Oh good, and that includes when you meet any of our specialists or councillors. Everyone, volunteers, administrators, specialists, that is to say ALL contribute our time and services free and that has been the way we have worked ever since we opened. Now,

Ann, just to get my notes right, your husband has just started his course for chemo?"

Ann found her voice. "Yes, he had his fourth session in Tembury Cancer Ward yesterday, and he is not taking it very well," she added.

"Well, when Sally, your consultant, arrives she will be most interested to get as many details as you can give her, to help her get a supporting picture," continued Jessie. "Now if you don't mind finding a seat for a few minutes, I will introduce you to Sally as soon as she arrives and she will take you to one of our interview rooms where it's comfortable and quiet."

Ann walked back into the big room and found a spare seat by a table full of magazines and the daily papers. She sat down and was forced to notice her finger nails once again. She curled her fingers into a ball on both hands so that she could avoid looking at the state of her nails. "I cannot believe it has only been ten days since the party," she recalled. How proud she had been of her hands and particularly her nails on her birthday. She thought back to the many occasions when women had complimented her on her slim fingers and beautifully shaped and manicured nails, remembering how so many of the guests had admired the lovely red, picking up the colour of her birthday party dress. Even John's brother's dreadful girlfriend had noticed and commented favourably, although her "How you manage your nails as well as looking after your two boys" felt then, as it did now, as a rather backhanded compliment!

Now look at them. Ann proceeded to glance at the chipped and broken nails. "What on earth would Carlotta at 'Bright Nails' think, or say, about my nails?" Ann shuddered to think and tried not to dwell on the almost non-stop series of problems which had crowded into her life.

Sitting quietly waiting for the consultant, Ann could not avoid going back over the awful events since her birthday celebrations. That very next morning the news that John needed urgent chemo for the prostate cancer to make sure the cancer did not migrate into his bones, and the boys being so upset when she had tried to explain that their dad was going to have some treatment at the cancer centre, and he might lose his hair. Then Harry burst into tears and the three of us cried, so scared that Dad, our dad, my husband, might not be all right, and there did not seem to be anything we could do but hope and pray.

Ann realised she was squeezing her bag as she thought of that stupid form teacher, what's his name? Pemdlebury, when he phoned up to say Harry was being 'obstructive' in the class. Ann thought back to that conversation as she tried to explain he was upset but thank goodness the year tutor had understood and was sympathetic but having to go into the school to explain all that, and then to try to talk to Harry, poor little soul!

Pamela broke into Ann's thoughts with, "I am so sorry, Ann, you are having to wait, it's so unlike Sally to be late for an appointment. Can I get you another cup of tea and we do have some lovely scones; Jane makes them for us all when she comes in, they really are scrumptious. You should try one."

"Well thank you but not this morning. I would however love another cup of tea, thank you so much," Ann replied. She sat thinking as the noise in the busy room seemed to fade away from her. "This is really the first time I have been on my own since before my birthday party. Well at least that went to plan," she thought ruefully. "Nothing much has since."

The tea arrived with Pamela. "I have finally got you a cup and saucer," she said triumphantly. "I just don't know where our consultant, Sally, is. Drink your tea and I will find out." And off she went to the reception area.

Ann was forced once again to consider the poor state of her nails as she sipped her tea. "What is the time?" she pondered. "I don't have to rush ... I can skip lunch ... I can't be late to pick up the boys. Whatever time this Sally person comes I should leave at, what, six thirty to get to the cancer clinic to see John. He will be waiting. I hate that place. I feel scared just going in. No, I must not think about the clinic like that and now Dad. I just cannot bear to think of him with this ghastly brain tumour waiting for the operation, who knows when, and on his own. I just feel so hopeless, so on my own."

"Hallo Ann, Jessie asked me to come across and explain the little problem we have with Sally, the consultant. Perhaps we could go into one of our interview rooms for a minute. I am a volunteer and my name is Daniel," smiling at her he indicated the label on his bright red jersey whilst taking the cup and saucer to carry it for her.

Daniel led the way past the standing visitors, through the door and beyond Jessie's office to a small comfortable interview room with two seats and a small table.

Putting Ann's cup of tea down, he said, "I am so sorry but Consultant Sally has had to cancel her meeting with you this morning. She wants me to express her real and sincere apology to you but her five year old daughter has had raging toothache and the only timescale she could get into dentist is in," and Daniel looked at his watch, "half an hour's time and unfortunately her client list requires her to be in London this afternoon. If you could pop in to Wellsbury Centre over the next week, she really will make your meeting a first priority."

Daniel looked at Ann in his open friendly way, sensitive to her feelings. Ann quickly responded. "Of course I understand perfectly. I have a five year old who needs a lot of my attention just now."

"Well, perhaps you can put up with me for a few minutes," Daniel laughed. "I have been coming in to do a shift for the centre for the last few years, well ever since I was cleared up from having the same trouble your husband is going through. Of course the treatments have moved on so much since my little episode."

Ann felt immediately comforted by talking to someone who had gone through John's experience and had clearly survived very well. "I will certainly tell John this evening, because you look especially fit and well."

"Well thank you, Ann, and I have just had a 'benchmark' birthday," replied Daniel.

Ann had to laugh. "Me too," she said, "when was your birthday?"

"On the twenty-fourth of this month," said Daniel.

"No!" exclaimed Ann. "That was the same day as me!! What a coincidence," and dropping her voice she said, "and I was forty – awful, I cannot bear the thought."

"Well," said Daniel, laughing at her, "you certainly do not look your 'awful' age, and I can double that…"

Ann's eyes widened in surprise and said, "You cannot possibly be eighty?!"

"Well there you are," Daniel continued in a light voice, "and we are both weathering well, despite my time 'before the mast' and the present stormy going for you. Now, since we are a 'special' birthday team, perhaps you would like to share with me how things are going for you. Just so you know, I have four children ranging from a bit older than you and a range of grandchildren, four of them matching your two boys' ages, so I'm fairly practiced at the practical and emotional ups and downs in youngsters lives."

Ann relaxed and found herself pouring out the whole story of her and John's shock at finding out he had serious cancer of the prostate the day after her birthday and the reaction of the boys, and the difficulties this had raised at the school. Plus the very next day the totally unexpected need for her dad to have a brain tumour removed and realising she could not be there with him as she felt she should because there was no one else to support him now.

She even found herself explaining how desperate she was feeling, because she was not able to organise herself as she always had, faced with supporting her husband, the boys, as well as her father and the job at the agency, whilst also feeling she was not able to look after herself.

This said, Ann glanced once again at her finger nails. Daniel followed her gaze and said, "Well, Ann, understandably everyone has looked to you as a tower of strength and organiser in the family and at the travel agent's, and they may not understand why you cannot give each of them the same attention that you have in the past. Now, perhaps I can help as we are a 'birthday' team, and I have had the advantage of managing teams of people, large and small for some time, so I have learned one or two 'wrinkles' that might help things along for you.

"Now, Ann, if you don't mind a couple of questions – Okay?"

Ann nodded.

"Excellent," said Daniel. "What time are you picking up the boys? – four thirty – fine, and going to see John? Seven – excellent. Now I notice your lovely hands and I can see you are not happy about your nails?"

Ann blushed. "No, I'm sorry, is it that obvious?" she almost whispered.

"No, not really," replied Daniel, "but I bet you go to 'Bright Nails' in the town and see Carlotta?"

Ann nodded in surprise. Daniel continued, "My wife tells me they really are the best nail specialists around and always busy."

"They certainly are, I had to take an appointment three days before my birthday," commented Ann.

"Do you mind if I pop out for a minute," said Daniel. "Just relax for a minute, I will be right back."

True to his word Daniel was back in no time. "Right," he said, "if you leave now and pop down to 'Bright Nails', Carlotta is happy to fit you in. My wife and Carlotta are great friends and Carlotta was delighted to support our 'team', particularly as you are a valued customer. Now that will give you plenty of time to pick up the boys and feel your best when you visit John this evening."

Ann felt too emotional to say anything but she hugged Daniel hard as she got to the door.

Daniel gave her a card and said, "Here is my business card with my mobile number. Call any time, just to chat if you would like to and I will be in the centre next Friday. Hope to see you then."

Later that evening Ann left a message on Daniel's mobile. "Just to tell you Dad has come through his op really well. I'm so relieved. The boys are fine and John said how good I was looking in my red dress, matching my nails which are the best I have ever had them. Thank you. Thank you Team Leader!! SEE YOU on Friday."

THE ANNUAL PERFORMANCE APPRAISAL

"Ah," said Mr Caldicote, "this is a fortunate meeting, and Mr Brenchley was going to give you a call. I see you are taking a file along, no doubt for Mr Beckworthy's office, and as I would not want to upset the Civil Service Head of Regional Services, please deliver that file first if you think you should do so!"

"No, I can drop this file in to Mr Beckworthy's secretary later if you wish to speak to me," said Ronald Brenchley in his usual, rather pedantic way.

Standing by his office door in the corridor of the executive suite, Mr Caldicote was, with one sweep of his arm, able to both open his glass panelled door and at the same time indicate the newly attached, and gold leafed resplendent label, pronouncing the office of 'Harold Caldicote, F.P.Inst.M, Head of Personnel Management and Development'. "Come in, Ron, and sit yourself down," he gushed.

Ronald moved into the spacious office with a view of other high rise city buildings and sat down on the seat in front of Mr Caldicote's desk, reflecting that his own office view from four floors down scarcely took in more than the roof of the public conveniences next to the civil service building.

"Lovely view isn't it, Ron? You don't mind me calling you Ron, do you?" and without waiting for a reply, Mr Caldicote went on. "Getting settled in to my new role here, I have decided to get to meet as many senior people as poss." Mr Caldicote said 'Get to meet' in the same way, thought Ronald, as one might say 'Catch you later' when you are in a hurry.

"Beginning with everyone in the department who has been here for some time so that with a face to face I get a real feel for the mood of the department, and of course the individuals, before I start the round of annual performance reviews" Mr Caldicote said, smiling comfortably at Ronald as he put his arms on the desk and put his fingers together like a steeple.

A somewhat confused Ronald could only clear his throat and say, "Yes."

"I see from the records," continued Mr Caldicote, "that you are one of our stalwarts with more time in the department than any other clerical grade?"

Ronald's only reasonable response seemed to be once again, "Yes."

"Well, Ron, since you and I have a moment," and at this point Mr Caldicote pulled out a file from the dozen or so stacked in what looked to Ronald like a supermarket trolley! "Not, of course, that I want today to get into the detail of your record with us," he said.

Ronald thought that was the sort of comment the Warden made to new prisoners entering a jail!

"I will be doing that…," and here Mr Caldicote checked his desktop computer. "…in a month or two," he eventually said. "But I thought you would appreciate having some indication of the areas I will be looking at when we have our little 'face to face'!"

After a pause, Ronald decided the only response that seemed appropriate was, "Yes."

Mr Caldicote flowed on smoothly, "Looking at my predecessor's comments on your last annual review". He turned over several buff coloured sheets entitled Civil Service Annual Review, without seeming to read the comments. "None the less," he said, "remarkable consistency." He then repeated to himself. "Remarkable consistency." He halted and then continued, "Your last three appraising managers seem to have had, well, universal agreement on your performance, remarkable, really". He shuffled the buff forms again before continuing.

"I very much doubt any other members of the department can boast of not a single unauthorised absence in ten years, and I know from your present manager, your timekeeping sets the standard for the whole unit. I also see that your work performance has consistently ticked the box for 'reliability, accurate and presented in 'A' grade form'."

"I see you and wife," and again Mr Caldicote glanced into the file, "Mabel, do not have any family. Not taken up golf?" He asked. Ronald's nod of the head satisfied him. "Sensible, a silly game. I spend hours looking for lost balls. I'm surprised we do not have any hobbies or interests listed down for you. Was that an oversight on our part?"

Ronald Brenchley considered the point for a minute or two, before he said, "No, not really."

Mr Caldicote persisted, convinced he was on to a departmental procedure failure. "Now Ron, you can't tell me you're not interested in food and wine," he said winningly. Again, Ronald gave the matter thought. "No, not really," he responded.

"Well," said a now slightly exasperated Mr Caldicote, "television, err … bird watching, stamp collecting. What do you do in the evenings when you leave work?"

Ronald's brow furrowed in concentration, before he said, "My wife always gets supper ready for my arrival home. We do have a nice piece of fish on Fridays. I read through the evening newspaper, and I feed the two gold fish."

"Ah," said Mr Caldicote triumphantly, "you have an interest in tropical fish?"

"No, not really," said Ronald, "they are my wife's. We did have three but one died." He paused for a moment. "On March the twelfth last year."

Exasperated, Mr Caldicot finally said, "Well thank you for sharing your time with me. It will," and he struggled to find the right words, "help when we come to your formal performance appraisal." As he ushered Ronald out of his office, at the same time his secretary entered. She became concerned to see Mr Caldicote sinking into his chair, mopping the perspiration from his brow with his handkerchief.

"Heaven help us, Mrs Hooper, I just hope we do not have any other members of staff as professionally pedestrian, totally lacking of ambition, and devoid of any outside interests as Mr Ronald Brenchley," he spluttered.

At twelve thirty-seven that afternoon Ronald was sitting in his customary April to October lunch time seat in the park opposite the civil service building, having already carefully wiped the wooden slats for pigeon droppings with the carefully folded duster, kept in a compartment in his lunch carrying briefcase.

Ronald usually took a minute to review the area weather forecast, and to scan the sky through the treetops, before finally going to his lunch venue. If it was raining, or threatening rain, he retreated across the small park to the 'Happy Eater Palace' that he frequented in the winter, where Carlo, always happy to see a regular client, would whisk out his own wooden chair and plant it on the end of the long shop window table, affording Ronald a regular 'bad weather' spot with a view back to the civil service building.

Carlo performed this service as he was then able to claim 'Senior Civil Service personnel use my Happy Eater all the time'.

On this particular day, Ronald might well have considered the slight mist in the air and the dark clouds overhead and made his way over to Carlo's. However, Ronald had been disturbed by the morning's chance meeting with Mr Caldicote, as he sat without even opening his briefcase to take out the thermos flask of tea, or the carefully packed sandwiches, whilst he carefully thought through Mr Caldicote's comments during the meeting.

Having carefully considered the points that had been made, and decided his responses had been quite appropriate, he still could not dispense a feeling of disquiet which bothered him.

That afternoon, and during his walk to the Underground from the civil service building, the feeling of disquiet grew without Ronald being able to put his finger on the reason.

'I mean,' thought Ronald, 'my life is properly organised, my home is just how I like it, Mabel knows exactly where I will be through the day and we are together in a quiet reading environment in the evenings. Although,' he thought, 'Mabel is inclined to read rather trashy novels nowadays!'

Ronald tried to comfort himself by reminding himself that, under civil service procedures he could retire in four years and seven months, having done service for the required thirty years.

Ronald also reflected he had held the same grade level for ten years; something of which to be proud. None the less, standing on the Underground platform waiting for the 5.27 p.m. train to arrive, he felt the weight of an unusual disturbance, perhaps an emotional feeling, upon him. When the train arrived he sat in the carriage with his briefcase on his lap, for the fifteen minute journey to his station, and ten minute walk to his home.

Still brooding on Mr Caldicote's remarks, or at least their implications, Ronald noticed sitting opposite him in the carriage were two young men talking animatedly with raised voices, and from their matching scarfs he presumed they were going to a local football match.

Ronald's daily Underground trips were often plagued by noisy travellers, and he generally took no notice, with his mind on other things. However, suddenly and quite unwittingly, one of the young men highlighted the very issue that had been bothering Ronald since his meeting with Mr Caldicote which was, he really did care about some things even if he did not express his concerns.

The young man, laughing with his mate, picked his nose. The unconscious action was completely without regard to the feelings of anyone within eyesight, and the fact that nobody took the slightest notice did not detract from Ronald's sudden feeling of irritation about the action.

Ronald Brenchley suddenly realised in a thunderclap of understanding why he had been so bothered by Mr Caldicote's comments. Mr Caldicote had decided Ronald was totally unresponsive and disinterested over anything that fell outside his ordered and disciplined life. This was not true, and this one minor incident in front of him brought home to him suddenly, all the irritating incidents he had seen but about which he suppressed his annoyance, refusing to allow the matters, small as they may be, to upset the order of his life.

Now, like turning on a hot tap, irritation flowed through his veins and with it disappeared the feeling of disquiet. He had to do something. He could scarcely wait to get home and he actually jogged the last thirty yards to his front door.

Mabel was coming down the stairs, hair brush in hand, as he swept through the door. She was almost open mouthed with surprise. "You're early dear." She was even more surprised and concerned when Ronald said, "I need to talk to you, Mabel."

Ronald ignored supper or slippers for the first time in their married life as he poured out, in careful detail, the events of the day from the meeting with Mr Caldicote to the Underground nose picking incident, and he even managed to explain the sudden realisation that he had been suppressing his feelings of irritation about the thoughtless, uncaring, disrespectful actions taken consciously, or unconsciously, by people who fall into his line of sight.

Mabel sat on the edge of her seat, initially scared by the measured intensity of Ronald's outpouring. Then as he warmed to the explanation, pleased to see a side of her husband that had never been on show before, Mabel became delighted that the door had finally been opened to Ronald's inner character. So long held shut by the personal rule of conduct which, she had decided years before, emanated from the single child upbringing with elderly parents, devoted to the Victorian ways of life, and a boys' public school which had tried, and failed, to achieve the status of a Minor Public School several times before cold showers and harsh disciplines finally caused its sudden demise just after Ronald had taken the Civil Service Entrance Exam and moved on.

Ronald suddenly stopped his, for him, extraordinary long explanation and expressed an interest in his supper.

Mabel said nothing as they shared boiled ham, baked potatoes and butter beans, but she thought deeply and pouring Ronald and her customary cup of tea, she said, "Ronald, I want you to write down these irritations you have observed and tomorrow I am going to buy you a little notebook you can carry with you in the inside pocket of your suit."

The tone, authority and unexpected nature of her statement caused Ronald to stop, with his teaspoon poised with two sugar lumps above his tea cup, as he contemplated his wife's thought, or as he saw it later, decision. His only response, which seemed appropriate was, "Yes, alright," as he dropped in the sugar lumps.

A day later as he took his customary journey to the civil service building, he had the comfortable feel of a rather smart notebook in the inner pocket of his suit jacket, and almost immediately he had an entry to make as he walked down the rather narrow Acacia Avenue where it was impossible for two cars to pass, mainly due to the residents' parked vehicles.

The school run mums, and occasional dads, had to travel the assault course every morning and afternoon. Some acknowledged the courtesy of other drivers, letting them through with the wave of a hand and a smile but most irritated Ronald, as he reflected back over the years, by storming through and ignoring the courtesy drivers, even finger pointing and horn blowing in their determination to get by.

Ronald stopped by the letter box and made a note.

Other incidents of 'intolerable irritations' soon began to fill pages of Ronald's notebook as he journeyed between home in Acacia Avenue and the civil service building.

No incident, however small, was missed.

Like on the Underground train, the office worker leaning on the support pole in front of him, chewing gum with an open mouth.

The queue jumpers, ignoring the shuffling line waiting to purchase a travel ticket.

The youth tossing an empty beer can towards the bin in the park, missing it and walking on regardless, and the stoic indifference by commuters on the Underground to the need of a frail old lady passenger standing with her walking stick, when a seat could be offered by someone, as Ronald always sought to do.

Entry after entry flowed, such as Ronald when having his cup of tea, with two sugars, observed the younger members of the civil service he knew well in the office, all sitting at their tables during the tea break, totally absorbed and isolated from each other, playing games on their computers, or communicating on their phones, without any thought or intention of engaging in the lightest conversation with each other on the state of the weather, or the nation.

Irritating incidents, carefully noted, began to fill up the notebook as Ronald journeyed on, now fully attentive to the thoughtless actions all around him.

After a couple of weeks of note taking that had enlivened Ronald's travels to and from work, attention that had even made the customary trip to the local supermarket with Mabel on Saturdays for the weekly shop, really rather enjoyable as he observed the shopping throng whilst he pushed along the trolley.

Mabel said at tea time on Sunday after two weeks, "I should like to see the notebook."

It seemed to Ronald to be more of a command than a request and so he obligingly passed over the notebook to Mabel. She started to read, carefully and steadily, as Ronald finished one cup of tea and a piece of her seed cake and she continued to read to the point that Ronald had to pour his own second cup, a most unusual occurrence.

Finally, Mabel looked at him over her reading glasses and said, "You have to explain."

Ronald considered her comments for some time without coming to a conclusion. "Explain what?" he said.

"What you are thinking when you see these inconsiderate irritations," said Mabel.

"Well," said Ronald, "I'm not sure I can."

"Of course you can," said Mabel firmly. "You just have to remind yourself of how you felt, when you saw, what you saw and make a note. Now, if you read your notes again and think back carefully, you will remember how you felt observing those little thoughtlessnesses."

Ronald wondered if there was such a word as 'thoughtlessnesses' and then decided if there wasn't, there should be! "Very well", he said.

Ronald's new found hobby filled him with a rather scary sense of purpose and he filled his tea breaks, lunch breaks and evenings, carefully noting irritating incidents and under Mabel's instruction, reflected on his reaction to the event. The more he thought about each event, the more it seemed to matter.

Ronald even bought a second note book, rather larger and with a nice blue plastic cover. He nearly bought one with a red cover but decided it was a step too far!

In the evenings he read his notebook filled with daily observations, and then sat and thought about each incident until he was sure he had caught his feelings at the time.

In Ronald's investigative phase, the tin can episode went from a single bright coloured empty beer can in the neatly cut grass of the park which was deliberately ignored by the alcoholic filled young miscreant, to what might happen to the park if all the people in the area thought it would be easier and cheaper to throw all their waste into this convenient open waste basket, rather than paying their council tax.

Ronald also considered how the acceptance of one discarded beer could lead to a collapse of the present community culture on matters of discarded waste.

Ronald found he was fascinated and, at the same time, depressed with his thoughts in the evenings.

Mabel made no comment as she made his breakfast, did his washing and ironed his shirts, prepared supper in the same methodical and careful way, as she had done for years.

Ronald maintained his daily routines, to, from and at the civil service building, apparently to his time honoured disciplines. However, under the surface, Ronald was now a man 'with a mission'.

"What," thought Ronald, "will be the results of the young of this country's devotion to electronic discourse, abbreviating the English language just to speed the electronic interactive dialogue, and now," thought Ronald, "the very seats of learning, the national schools are allowing, even encouraging lessons and homework to be completed electronically." "Isn't it inevitable," Ronald thought, "that generations to come will only know how to communicate, face to face, in a monosyllabic abbreviated form of English, quite incomprehensible to their parents or the older generation? What kind of world will that be?"

And then one day the adventure stopped. Ronald came home having not seen a single new incident of ill-considered irritability to mark in his notebook, and his enthusiasm to explain how he felt about what he had seen evaporated that evening, just as abruptly.

Ronald placed both books on the Sitting Room mantelpiece between the sturdy 'H.Morrison Chiming Clock' that his mother had left him with a page of hand-written instructions on winding up and setting the date dial, and the elaborately figured and coloured Victorian flower vase that Mabel had unexpectedly purchased whilst visiting the recently departed old lady's house contents sale at number five Acacia Avenue.

Life quickly returned to the normal, daily routine. Ronald made his steady way between home and the civil service office. His workload remained steady in the office and the investigative interest that had been part of his daily activity for a few short weeks faded from his mind, as his lifelong routines took their customary hold on his days.

Ronald did notice the notebooks had disappeared from the sitting room mantelpiece a few days after his project had come to an end, but he decided that Mabel had put them tidily away somewhere, or disposed of them in her tidy way.

The day arrived when Ronald's office computer messaged his annual appraisal interview was scheduled for Monday the following week. Ronald read the diary message and his heart sank as he ran through the incvitable series of questions from Mr Caldicote, now clearly going to be more pointed than the discussion at their preliminary meeting.

Ronald could already hear the inevitable criticism of his continued lack of outside interests or his continued refusal to take any steps to improve his career in the civil service during the last year.

On his way home Ronald had the uncomfortable feeling that the pressure he was feeling just behind his eyes, was a prelude to the unpleasant feeling of 'disquiet' which had enveloped him only a few weeks ago.

When Ronald arrived home, he sat in his armchair without even bothering to change his office shoes for slippers as he explained to Mabel that he was commanded to face Mr Caldicote on the following Monday at nine o'clock precisely for his annual performance review.

Mabel listened and then said, "I see," without further comment which surprised and depressed Ronald somewhat.

The next couple of days Ronald's feeling of disquiet developed into a full scale headache to the point that when he arrived in for supper on Wednesday, he was seriously wondering if he shouldn't put in a Form E.R.F/9712/B which he knew had to be processed to apply for early retirement, and to do this rather than face the 'inquisition' of Mr Caldicote and his annual appraisal.

Ronald did not feel up to sharing this step with Mabel but he did acquire the form from personnel the next morning.

On Wednesday Ronald arrived home to find a large, highly polished limousine, parked outside with a uniformed driver sitting inside.

Anxiously Ronald put his key in the door but it was opened before he had time to turn the key, by Mabel in her very best dress, holding a glass of champagne. Not, considered Ronald, a greeting he had enjoyed for many years.

"Come in, Ronald dear, and meet Mr Gillespie from Universal Publishing," Mabel said in an excited voice.

Ronald walked in a daze into the sitting room where a somewhat earnest looking, bespectacled business man, shook him firmly by the hand with an "It's a real honour to meet you, sir", and "We very much look forward to seeing you and your wife as our guests on Friday".

The business man continued. "I hope you will forgive me if I slip off now to ensure all the arrangements are in place. I can tell you Ronald, may I call you Ronald? – my name is Philip, here is my card, that the Universal Publishing team feel we have never had such a good chance of collecting a national award, thanks to your work," He then left a folder of papers on the table as he moved towards the door.

"Goodbye, Mabel, and thank you for all your help. I will see myself out and I can assure you both the car will be here in plenty of time to get you to your hotel to get settled in before the event. You have my mobile number so just call for anything, anything you, Ronald, might need." He finished, smiling.

With that Philip was gone and Ronald in a state of bemused stupor, listened to the sound of the limousine moving away down Acacia Avenue.

Mabel poured out a glass of champagne and thrust it into Ronald's hand. She said, "Sit down, Ronald dear. Let me explain. I sent your two notebooks to the commissioning editor at Universal Publishing, because I thought the things you had written about 'Intolerant Irritations' were important. I didn't say anything to you because I did not want to disappoint you as I knew you were anxious about things."

"Well, anyway, within no time I had a phone call to say they were really interested in publishing your book, which they are now scheduling to promote nationwide next month, and it seems from the contract Phil went through with me, and has left for us to consider, your book will give us a tidy sum once they print as well as, potentially, a great deal of commission in the future. Particularly so now," continued Mabel, "as the 'powers that be' at Universal Publishing have submitted your manuscript as their entry for this year's 'New Fiction, New Writer of the Year' awards."

"And," added Mabel almost beside herself with excitement, "your manuscript has been selected as one of the three to be judged this Friday evening on television at the Grosvenor Hotel, where," added Mabel having taken a further gulp of the champagne, "Philip has arranged a suite for us to stay in and during the selection process you will be seen on national television."

Ronald sipped his champagne and thought.

Mabel continued. "I went out and bought you a really lovely new suit, a shirt and a tie. Well we can certainly afford it now, and I knew you would want to look your best on Friday."

Ronald had yet to consider what being on television might be like, but he was seriously wondering what Mr Caldicote would make of his appearance and how that might influence his annual performance appraisal on Monday!

THE COLLECTING TIN

Thomas Major looked carefully at the shirt shelves in his suit cupboard. Each of the neatly stacked shirts all in their colour groups met his approval. He reminded himself he would thank Mrs Hetheringill when she brought his next batch of neatly ironed washing next Tuesday.

Selecting a pale blue shirt and a dark blue tie, Mr Major, as he liked to be known, spent some time choosing a medium weight tailored suit, thinking as he did so that his appearance at the Old Boy's Lunch had to fit the pattern he had managed over several years to present himself to his old school colleagues as a retired, highly successful, accountant, who was using his many skills to develop new connections now that he had time to do so.

Making sure that during any lunch discussions he could avoid the embarrassment as being remembered as having two left feet in any sports activity as when the sports master famously commented that he "ran like a ruptured duck". Memories that the back slapping members remember 'that goal I scored in the House final' brigade liked to recall, or the 'glad to see you are maintaining your handicap again this year' golf group, who noisily dominate the lunch, liked to laugh about.

Mr Major sighed as he looked in the mirror, making sure his tie knot was perfectly central to the collar. If only one or two of his valuable old tax clients were not going to be present at the Old Boy's Lunch, he could dodge the whole event.

Switching his mind to the comfortable thought that he could enjoy an evening listening to classical music on his splendid, if a little expensive, new music centre, and then next week back to his carefully organised routine where his 'professional veneer' as Mr Major liked to think of it, kept him nicely isolated from the noisy, interfering, messy, disorganised, untidy aspects of life which Mr Major felt crowded in on him whenever he let his guard down for a moment. He reminded himself how fortunate he was not taking on any of the accounting roles he had been encouraged to take in charitable organisations when it was known he had retired.

Now ready to leave, Mr Major mentally ticked off watch, diary, gold pen, clean handkerchief, a little change to purchase his daily paper. This reminded him, his charity tin in which he deposited his minor change every evening, was full and needed to be dropped off at the local hospice where he would need to pick up an empty collecting tin. He thought, as he glanced at his watch, plenty of time to do that on his way to the wretched lunch.

In the car Mr Major reflected, with some pleasure, how he ensured his regular charitable full tin gift to the local hospice fitted so nicely into his carefully crafted image of the successful retired professional, generously giving to his community. He had to admit driving along, that the time when he had noted down, and then added up, every small change coin he had put into the tin, the total sum had not added up to much, but he was comforted with the thought that locals seeing him regularly turn up with the tin would not know the actual value in the tin that he was contributing towards the running costs of the hospice.

Mr Major parked the car in the hospice car park and rather ostentatiously swinging the bright blue tin from its string, walked into reception. "Good morning," he said to the volunteer receptionist, with a badge which proclaimed that role and her name, 'Peggy'.

"I have come," Mr Major said, rather unnecessarily, "to leave my gift collecting tin. I have marked my name and address on the label," and he added, largely for the benefit of the half a dozen people sitting anxiously in the waiting area, "I would like an empty replacement tin please ... Peggy."

"Of course, Mr Major," said Peggy. "Thank you so much for helping the hospice work keep going here in the community." Nicely put, thought Mr Major.

"Unfortunately I have no spare tins with me here in reception, and as you can see we are quite busy this morning. I will need to phone down to the office to get a tin for you, if you could wait for a few minutes."

"Of course, Peggy," said Mr Major.

"It's a little crowded here and so perhaps you would like to go out to our Garden of Remembrance," said Peggy. "It's very nice out there and one of our patients has also just gone to look at the flowers."

Mr Major wandered into the remembrance garden through the rose arbour, impressed with the neat paths and flower beds with seat bowers covered with climbing roses, where two people could sit and talk privately without being overlooked.

Mr Major, who had never ventured beyond the reception desk at the hospice over his three or four visits with his collecting tin each year, realised that the private seats in the commemorative garden might afford the opportunity for families to say their final goodbyes to those patients who had come into the hospice to die. A process that Mr Major had never considered before as he walked amongst the flower beds and rose covered seats.

Mr Major sat down in the next rose arbour, suddenly conscious he had never considered his own death and linking these considerations with the thought that he might need the hospice to help him through his own last days. His reverie was disturbed by the sound of a voice coming from behind him and Mr Major realised that someone was sitting in the rose arbour that was back to back to his own.

The voice was that of a man, steady but clearly very upset. Mr Major decided the bower must be filled by the patient in the hospice.

"Where are you, where can you be, why have you not replied to any of my letters, this is the end for me. Surely you could just give me the chance to make my peace with you before I go. I have no one in my life to mourn me and I am so alone." The voice tailed away into deep sobs.

A very uncomfortable Mr Major hurried back to reception to be offered an empty collecting tin by Peggy.

Rather awkwardly, Mr Major said, "I think the gentleman, your patient in the garden, is very upset. I did not want to disturb him but I thought you should know."

"Oh thank you, Mr Major," replied Peggy. "I will get a nurse to pop out to be with him. Unfortunately Mr Arnold Hunt has no family as far as we know and he is very lonely here in his last few days with us."

The lunch went as well and as badly as Mr Major had anticipated. He kept himself to himself with undue embarrassment and made the minimum courteous responses when called to do so without having to reveal any details of his private and individual lifestyle in the course of the limited social chit chat that he was obliged to undertake.

Undoubtedly some of Mr Major's concentration was distracted by running the sad voice of Arnold Hunt in his rose arbour over and over in his head but if anything his rather distant demeanour seemed to make it easier to drift through lunch without the bother of being socially attentive.

Somehow the look forward to music evening with a glass or two of sauvignon blanc was not as enjoyable as Mr Major had planned and he went to bed having disposed of the whole bottle of wine with the sound of Arnold Hunt's sad voice still in his head.

At some time in the dark hours of the night, Thomas Major heard his mother's voice.

"Thomas, come to the window."

He could hear her very clearly and he knew he had to do what she asked, as he had always done. He went to the window and his mother's voice said, "Open the window, Thomas, and look out."

Thomas opened the window and looked out over the garden. Only there was no garden. Just a long, long, grey corridor which stretched away into the black distance of oblivion further than his eyes could see.

"Who do you see through the window, Thomas?" his mother's voice asked.

"I see no one, Mother," said Thomas.

"And that is because you have no one in your life, Thomas," said his mother.

Thomas Major woke with a terrible start, sweating from every pore, standing in front of his suit cupboard with his hand on the open door. He slept no more that night but by nine o'clock with a cup of tea and a shower, he was dressed, if casually for him, and from a plan formed in his high state of anxiety he was as ready as he could ever be to return to the hospice.

When Thomas arrived he explained to the receptionist on duty, Jane, that he was here to visit Mr Arnold Hunt. He was, he explained, a very old acquaintance who had heard that Arnold had not had any visitors and being local he thought he would drop in to see him.

Standing in the reception Thomas did not even consider the significance of his completely fabricated story, a matter which only a day ago would have horrified him. He just knew he needed to meet and talk to Arnold Hunt.

After a short delay a pleasant young nurse showed Thomas into Arnold's small room where he was propped up in bed with a large white pillow, that Thomas was very aware highlighted the grey complexion and white wispy hair of the dying man, looking much older than his years. A man who was now staring at Thomas in obvious confusion.

"The nurse said we know each other. I'm awfully sorry but I cannot recall our acquaintance, or where we knew each other but please forgive me I really am not myself nowadays," Arnold said in a quiet voice.

"No, Mr Hunt, please forgive me. We have never met, well not directly but I was in the Garden of Remembrance yesterday and I overheard you talking – eh, quite by accident, I assure you. Please forgive me, I heard you saying you were on your own here in the hospice and as I come here occasionally, for other reasons, I thought you might not object if I just popped in to see you." Thomas blurted out, a little embarrassed.

"How very kind of you. What a surprise. I think you already know my name – Arnold. May I enquire of yours?"

"Thomas Major. – Thomas," he replied as he sat down in the comfortable seat by Arnold's bed.

To Thomas's complete surprise he found himself inventing a completely new personality, exaggerating his interests in music and the arts and implying a family, located abroad, but family none the less.

Arnold visibly relaxed in his hospice bed and his demeanour changed as he explained to Thomas that he had been an accountant until he retired and had been very focused upon his career and making money in his own business which was why, he explained to Thomas, he had so few friends and why his wife left some years ago having blamed him. "Correctly as I now see it," added Arnold, "for ignoring her and any of her interests."

"Sadly," continued Arnold, "I was never able to at least make things up to her before cancer took her and," said Arnold sadly, "our only daughter totally took her side and after her mother's death she simply moved to the Midlands and disappeared from my life, my fault entirely. Now please, you have been kind enough to come and spend a little time with me, tell me about yourself."

Thomas expanded upon his alter ego 'world' surprisingly easily and with a promise to visit for an hour the next day, a suggestion received with a tired enthusiasm by Arnold, Thomas left having first enquired if it would be in order for him to drop by the next day.

The ward sister agreed to his next day visit, although she stressed that Arnold was not long for this world.

By the next morning, after a very disturbed night, Thomas had formulated a plan and in his careful way worked out the steps he felt would be required.

Arriving at Arnold's bedside with a copy of the latest Accountant Institute Magazine, having carefully avoided any mention that they had both been in the same profession, Thomas broached the first step of his strategy, and without overly pressing for information from Arnold found out that his daughter had qualified as an accountant and his late wife had mentioned the Birmingham area some years before when the subject of his daughter's location was mentioned.

Under some gentle questioning, the daughter's name was shared, Emily Louise, an old fashioned name, although Arnold had no idea whether she was married or not so her surname was a mystery.

By the next morning Thomas had listed the telephone numbers of every accounting firm in the Birmingham district and by methodically calling and asking to speak to

'Emily Louise', after more than twenty fruitless calls, he was put through to Arnold's daughter in the accountancy practice.

The next part of Thomas's careful and practical plan slipped into place. He explained he was an old friend of her father and by implication suggested her father was aware of where his daughter practised as an accountant, and went on to explain that her father was dying in the hospice and he was now too ill to call as he sincerely wished, realising he had let his daughter down all her life, to make his peace if only for a few minutes, if that were possible, and was anxious to provide a car to collect her and return her to her home in Birmingham if she could spare an hour or two before he passed away.

There was a long silence from Emily Louise on the end of the line but suddenly she agreed to come down from Birmingham. To Thomas's surprise she would bring her five year old son, Harry, to see his grandfather before it was all too late.

Arrangements were made and agreed and at eleven o'clock the next day a very apprehensive Thomas poked his head round Arnold's bedroom door and eased into the room with a large parcel under his arm.

Arnold was gradually able to focus upon the day and visibly perked up at seeing Thomas in his room. Seated by the bed Thomas held Arnold's hand as he quietly explained that he had found, and talked to, Emily Louise and she was visiting in a few minutes to see him and was bringing his grandson to meet his grandfather. Information Arnold received, wide eyed with amazement, but without any comment.

As Thomas had arranged, a nurse arrived into the room with a cheerful bowl of fresh flowers and a tray of soft drinks to ensure that Arnold would be caught up in the flow of events.

In fact Arnold gathered himself rather well, rising to the occasion, and put on his dressing gown with some help, and composed himself in his bedside chair before the door opened and the hospice receptionist ushered in Arnold's daughter Emily Louse and Harry, his little wide-eyed grandson, holding his mother in one hand and a model aeroplane in the other.

Leaving Harry with his large parcel seated on the carpet at his grandfather's feet, Thomas backed out of the door, almost overwhelmed with emotion in the room as father and daughter embraced each other.

Thomas, the ward nurse and an orderly waited at the end of the corridor, ready to go back into the room if needed.

Half an hour later Arnold, holding on to his daughter's arm, came slowly into the corridor led by a small beaming Harry, carrying a box of Mechano almost as big as he was, with his toy aeroplane.

It was clear for all to see that family harmony had been recovered and so it was.

The very next day Thomas went to the hospice reception desk to visit Arnold, hopeful that he was happy over the surprise visit, only to be told by Peggy, that sadly Arnold had passed away at four o'clock that morning. This said, she handed Thomas an envelope with the words, 'For the attention of Thomas Major, Esq' a little shakily penned but clear none the less.

Thomas went into the remembrance garden and found the rose arbour where only a few days ago he had heard the sad voice of Arnold calling out his loneliness at the end of his life. He opened the envelope, the note inside was brief. 'My dear Thomas, your fine opened spirited and caring concern for me, a total stranger, finding my daughter and my lovely grandson, has allowed me to pass away in total peace. I cannot express my gratitude in words and I know my daughter will keep in touch with you if you will allow enough time for her in your busy life, when you so generously give of your time to help and support others not as fortunate as yourself, with my highest admiration and thanks. Arnold Hunt'

"Peggy, I wonder if you could enquire if the administration could spare me a minute or two," Thomas asked when returning to the reception area.

A matter of minutes later Thomas found himself with a cup of tea, sitting in the administrator's office. "I am so sorry you had to wait to get your collecting tin, Mr Major, we really do appreciate your regular contributions to our fund."

"No, no, really that is not why I am here. I would very much like you to accept me as one of your volunteers to come in to talk to any of the patients who come into your hospice at the end of their life and are perhaps on their own. Although they will receive, as they all do such care and careful medical support to ease their remaining days."

The administrator smiled. "I understand Mr Major you are a leading professional in the accounting world. Would you have the time to give us here at the hospice?"

Thomas's response was quick and honest. "Thanks to recent events I have been able to think through what should be the priorities in my life and I have also been able to reorganise my time, and I would now be able to respond to a call from your staff any day. Indeed, any time during the day, during the week, and with my new found experience of your services I am sure that I can contribute. Also being close by, I can visit any patient who may not have family support during their last few days."

Thomas continued to explain his reason for the discussion with the administrator. "I have led a carefully managed and structured lifestyle, perhaps too much so, but I can assure you that with your support I can switch these skills as a volunteer visitor member of your hospice organisation and I am ready today to do so from today."

With a beaming smile the administrator said with an outstretched hand. "Welcome aboard, Thomas, we will be delighted to have you as a member of the hospice team, ready to take your new place and offer a personal, warm, friendly and supportive relationship to everyone who comes to the hospice for help."

THE FIRST DAY AT WORK

"You are not going out in that jumper?" came the sharp remark.

"Oh, for goodness sake I am not going to change, I mean who is going to see me, a voluntary driver in my car? I am taking them for Mrs Blake's hospital appointment. I should have thought they will just be grateful I turn up," came the equally sharp retort.

"That's not the point, William," said Joy. He always knew she was annoyed, or concerned, when she called him 'William'.

"You are lucky to get this voluntary job and I will not have people reporting back to 'Dial-A-Car' what a messy driver they had on your first job."

"Oh, Okay, I will change my jumper," Bill said, wearily and then sarcastically. "Is there anything else you want, clean and polish the car again before I leave?"

"Don't be silly, Bill," Joy said in a quiet voice. "I want you to enjoy the experience and I'm sure when you get to meet people and you are helping them to their hospital and NHS specialists' appointments, you will find it very interesting. A whole new world and at least you will not be sitting around waiting for the pub to open, like your friend Jimmy. He's not going to last long now he's retired, and I want you to go on picking up your pension from that miserable company until you are at least ninety."

Bill looked at himself in the mirror, now in his last Christmas blue cardigan. He supposed he did look more tidy, even he thought, rather professional with his blue slacks and blue button down shirt and Joy was right, Jimmy had put on a lot of weight in the short time he had been retired and he did seem to have slowed down and less interested in anything much other than the next TV football match.

Bill checked the pink contact slip form 'Dial-A-Car', the co-ordinating agency where he had signed up to take local people for their NHS appointments. He slipped the petrol chit covering the sixty mile round trip in the glove box, with the contributors' envelope that clearly indicated the need for the couple being ferried to their appointment to deposit ten pounds towards the costs.

Finally settled to the job in hand, Bill put the car into gear, making sure that the direction sheet he had carefully worked out to get to the Blakes' home in the village a few miles away was on hand, he checked his watch to remind himself he had more than enough time to pick the Blakes up and get them to the out-patients clinic at St Stephens in time for their appointment.

Turning out of the crescent on to the main road, Bill thought. "What a difference. Here I am actually doing something which might help people only a couple of weeks after spending a working lifetime helping that wretched insurance company not to help people whenever and however they could. A slave to their management control procedures – 'Designed to help you get the best benefit from your Insurance Claim' as that ghastly jingle went"!

Bill concentrated upon the traffic lights wanting them to go green, so he could concentrate on anything that would stop the hated jingle in his head again, and again.

Back on the move, Bill thought as he had many times in the two weeks since his retirement, how often he had followed the insurance 'guidance' and squeezed the claimants who were unfortunate enough to need recompense for items damaged, lost, or stolen, always starting out feeling that their insurance cover would help them over their claims. The more Bill thought about it as he drove along, the more despondent he became as he remembered those 'weasel words' and phrases in letters, and the more uncomfortable he became as he drove.

"Was I really so uncaring over people's difficulties and genuine needs that I simply followed the wretched company 'Customer Care Response' procedures?" pondered Bill.

Bill circumvented a traffic island, carefully avoiding a cyclist resplendently dressed in green Lycra pants, a yellow reflective jacket and a large protruding 'Go Fast' helmet combined with three flashing lights on the bike, which made Bill think of a mobile Christmas tree, and giving the cyclist a wide berth as he eased the car past.

Bill recalled he had brought up the 'unfairness' of company procedures at one of those early staff 'get together' sessions beloved by the top brass and "a fat lot of good it did me", he thought. "What was it that guy from the head office branch said, Oh yes … 'Well William, looking at your last year's bonus I see you have benefitted directly from keeping a lid on our claims payments and your boss tells me you're one of our most able operators in dealing with claim responses, and you know, William, we all understand one of the truths about human nature is that virtually all claimants push their claim up when they put their claims forward, so well done, keep the good work up, Bill'."

"I suppose I just gave up, and shut up," thought Bill, stopping the car to wait whilst a mother pushing a small perambulator with a large bag of groceries hitched on the back handle, crossed the zebra crossing.

"That's the real world," thought Bill. "I bet that lady has to scrimp and save to make sure her kid has all the right food for him, or her, and here I am without a family to support except Joy, and comfortably off thanks to making sure that people got the minimum from their insurance claims – what a testimonial to be remembered by!!"

Bill drove steadily, attentive to the road and his route, while his mind wandered dismally on his role at the Insurance Training Centre. Memories like neon book marks, word perfect, kept flashing through his mind such as, 'We have noted in your claim that you have omitted the formal refurbishment estimate required for our assessor to consider your claim. You will see from Clause 14, paragraph 3 of your 'Economy Insurance' contract with us, that this eliminates items 1 to 4 and 7 to 9 of your claim. We are pleased to enclose a cheque for the balance of the items referred to under your claim.'

Thought after thought crowded in on Bill. 'Your policy specifically requires your detailed claim to be submitted on Claim Form 127/NC/A Part 2 within seven days of your advising us of the loss. We are sorry therefore that your claim cannot be processed on this occasion.'

Driving along Bill knew he could recall dozens of standard responses provided by the insurance company to cover almost any set of circumstances presented by the claimants.

"All these clever little procedures," thought Bill bitterly, "simply designed to delay, reduce or eliminate claims, and I followed them slavishly for years."

Bill turned the car left by the supermarket and went down Beech Green Road to No. 27, on the left of the road. He turned the engine off and sat looking at the front of No. 27. Neat, tidy, with yellow curtains at the windows to the left and right of the green front door.

"I must get rid of this depressing mood," thought Bill, glancing at his watch, five minutes to the pick-up time. "Okay, concentrate upon the future. I could take some lessons and learn to play the piano. I was quite good on the mouth organ when I was a kid, or take up painting?"

The front door opened and a gentleman in a raincoat waved to Bill, beckoning him into the house.

Bill locked the car and walked the few steps from the front gate to be greeted by a cheerful Mr Blake, or Henry as he liked to be known.

"My wife, Rosemary," explained Henry, "will be a few minutes getting ready to come with us as she has some bone deformity in her foot and needs time to get her shoe on. It's why we visit the specialist. It's so kind of you to pick us up, and right on time. Unfortunately Rosemary's foot does not let her walk all the way to the bus stop and so the Dial-A-Car service really is a godsend."

"Ah here's Rosemary," said Henry turning towards a small lady coming towards him. "Rosemary, this is our splendid driver, eh?"

"Bill," said Bill.

"Oh thank you, yes, Bill, who is so kindly driving us to St Stephens this afternoon," Henry concluded, giving Bill a warm smile.

By the time Bill had got the front door locked to Henry's satisfaction and the Blakes settled in the car, a companionable feeling had quite dissipated the dark depression which had hung over him on his arrival.

It turned out that Henry was an excellent navigator, carefully calling every turn and road obstruction on the Blakes' often undertaken route to St Stephens so that they arrived nicely early, and Bill was gratified to have the praises of Henry and Rosemary for the 'smooth' trip they had experienced. Apparently not always the case with Dial-A-Car drivers!

Bill therefore was in an excellent frame of mind as he made his way to St Stephen's coffee shop, having assured the Blakes he would be in the car in half an hour in plenty of time to take them home, upon Henry's assurance that the specialist would give his wife twenty minutes 'to the dot' and they would have to wait at least half an hour in the queue for their appointment.

In the coffee shop, Bill had just settled with his medium latte when he was hailed by a smiley faced individual who said, "Hi, I saw your Dial-A-Car sticker on your motor. I'm here in the same 'game', my name's Terry," and proffered his hand to Bill.

Bill, pleased to have company, made space for Terry and they set to chat once Bill had explained it as his first day on the job.

"Been doing it over a year now," said Terry, "fills in the empty spaces in my painting and decorating job and although it really only covers the cost of bringing the punters to an appointment, occasionally it throws up a chance for a bit of decorating, and so I feel I'm doing something a bit worthwhile and keeping myself going at the same time … how about you, Bill?"

"Well to be honest, I'm here because my wife nagged me to do something as I have just retired from an office job and she thought I might sit around and drink too much and spend the afternoons watching TV … and she might be right. Anyhow I am shipping a very nice old couple and better get back to them." As he got up, Bill turned to Terry and said, "You got a card, you never know I might meet someone who wants a bit of decorating done? Better still, I bet Joy is thinking now I'm about I can redecorate the kitchen and I'm hopeless and don't like doing it, so perhaps we can work something out!"

Terry produced a card from his wallet and with a handshake they went on their separate ways.

True to his prediction, Henry arrived back with Rosemary at Bill's car spot on time. Rosemary chatted about the nice specialist's talk with her. About why the NHS could now provide the special orthopaedic shoe which would help her to walk on the trip back to Beech Green Road.

On arriving at No. 27, Henry and Rosemary sought to persuade Bill to join them for a cup of tea and one of Rosemary's special scones. "A regular winner at the Women's Institute Annual Food Fair," said Henry, pressing Bill to accept the invitation.

Bill found himself sitting around the table in the Blakes' small but immaculate kitchen while the kettle boiled and Rosemary laid out the scones and strawberry jam.

"Sorry we are not in our drawing room," said Henry, "but it's a mess since the accident."

"Oh, I'm sorry," said Bill, "what sort of accident did you have?"

"A water pipe joint on the hot water tank went in the roof a couple of weeks ago. Of course we are insured but it seems that we have 'limited' cover and it looks as if we will have to spend the money we had put by to have Rosemary's special shoe made, to cover most of the damage," Henry replied.

"Oh well," said Rosemary, "we are no worse off and we did not really understand all the clauses in our insurance when we took the 'Economy Insurance' cover, thinking we would save money and be well insured."

Ever since the matter of insurance had come up, Bill had been holding his cup of tea getting more concerned by the second. Then suddenly his mood changed and he thought, "Wait a minute, this is where I can help these good people."

"Henry, I wonder if you mind showing me your letter and cover note from the insurance company but before you do so do you mind showing me the damage in your drawing room?" said Bill, putting his cup down.

Once they were back in the kitchen Henry duly produced the letter, as Bill had guessed from his old employers and was phrased exactly as Bill expected. He said to them, "Rosemary, Henry, if you would allow me I think I might be able to help you. You see, until recently I was involved in the insurance profession and so I understand the way things work." The Blakes nodded in unison, relieved that someone understood their difficulties.

Bill went on. "Okay, now I am going to draft out a reply for you to send back, Henry, in your own hand and I'm going to give you the name of a very nice painter and decorator who I will get to call on you to give an estimate. We will wait until you have a reply to your letter, which I predict will arrive promptly on Wednesday, if you get your reply in the post tomorrow, Henry."

"Now," continued Bill, "the only other thing is, I will call into 'Carpet Cover' in the High Street and ask their salesman to come down and give you a formal estimate to replace all your drawing room carpet because that is also covered under your policy, and next Wednesday, when we have the insurance company's response, we will send in all the replacement costs. You are well covered, despite all the small print clauses that insurance people like to confuse you with."

"I hope, Henry, you can read my writing as it's very important you put down exactly what I have drafted out," Bill said. "Rosemary, I suggest you get on getting your special shoe measured up as I promise you, you will not need to touch your savings as the water damage in your drawing room will all be put right and paid for by your insurance company."

Joy was looking anxious as Bill arrived home. "I was worried, you are so late." To which Bill responded cheerfully, "Well, I had a busy first day driving the Blakes and I will be helping them again next week. I think I am going to enjoy my new career."

WHAT'S IT ALL ABOUT?

Standing outside the St George's Chapel "Enter through the door" sign with my coat collar turned up, I was grateful that I had wrapped my best grey scarf around my neck although rather wishing I had a decent hat to wear for such an occasion. Anyhow I was here ... of course I was ... to respect the parting of my old, well now I can say, friend!

Standing there as much as possible out of the wind, I thought back to the beginning of our friendship.

I recalled I had seen Ronald several times at the Rec, watching the Roxborough Under 18 Boys Football team battling out their Saturday morning fixture with Reg, their trainer, and a few of the boys' dads in attendance.

That year, now four years ago, the team were doing well in the county's Under 18 league, and I had got used to going on the team bus to the away games as Reg knew I was a reliable, regular supporter. Not like many of the dads who only turned up to home games, when it wasn't raining!

Well, as luck would have it, Ronald got on the coach for an away game and sat next to me.

I recalled I immediately liked his style. He didn't ask me any questions, which I hate, and we just exchanged a couple of pleasantries on the trip.

The boys played really well, and as I remember went home cheerfully singing "We are the champions" on their way to finishing top of the league that season.

Ronald and I got used to chatting about the game and other things over the stop for "fish and chips" tradition for our away games, without ever asking questions about our lives outside the team support, a comfortable situation we both liked.

Anyway, from then on we pretty much met every Saturday morning during the rest of the season.

We did quite often talk about the state of the country, including immigration, lack of political leadership, and the weather. I recall him saying, "Where is the next Margaret Thatcher?", although neither he, nor I, ever indicated if we voted red, blue, green or any other colour in an election.

Of course I do remember the Saturday just before the end of the first season when we had met, actually the very last game. We had both been invited by Reg to join the team celebration supper at the Dog & Drake pub in the village. Apparently somebody had sponsored the whole evening and we had both agreed to join in.

At the game, however, Ronald told me he would not be able to make the pub event. Naturally I did not ask why but he told me anyway. It was something to do, he said, with his daughter. I knew she was his only child and like me, he was a widower.

To my surprise he continued on and although he spoke steadily, I could tell he was quite emotional. "Yes," he said, "my daughter is moving to America to one of the southern states, with my two grandchildren and I will be saying goodbye to them on the day of the football club celebration."

Apart from saying how sorry I was he was not able to be with the team, I remember I thought he would not mind if I shared my own way of dealing with my daughter, and my grandson and granddaughter, who all live in New Zealand, and as I found out later were coincidentally exactly the same age as Ronald's grandson and granddaughter.

Anyway, I remember I presumed to say to him that from my experience, "A regular exchange of telephone conversations once a week, although expensive, is a good way of keeping in touch and the grandchildren write to me once a month and send the occasional photo of their school and sports events. I always write back. Not, of course, the same as visiting them which is well outside the size of my pocket, but goes some way to bridge the gap between us."

I hoped my comments were supportive and he would not think I was presuming upon his privacy. He did not seem to take my comments amiss and as I thought about it, I realised I would not be meeting him again until, or perhaps because of, the upsetting news Ronald had just shared with me, I took the bull by the horns and asked him if he would like to come to the Working Men's Club in the town next Saturday afternoon, as I am a member, for a pot of tea now we did not have our morning game to follow.

I am fairly sure I said their afternoon tea was considered to be the best in the town and the scones and cakes on offer are well worth saving the pennies for. I certainly did not say "and you can tell me about how the goodbye event went with your grandchildren." That would have crossed the comfort line of our relationship.

I remember he responded by saying, "I'll be there at three if that is convenient," in his gentlemanly way, and then quite surprisingly shook me by the hand.

Thinking back I remember being quite anxious waiting for him to visit the Working Men's Club the next Saturday.

I was walking around the entrance foyer of the club, worried that he might not turn up but there he was smack on three o'clock as I had suggested and with his football scarf round his neck, which made me feel a trifle undressed, I remember.

Tea went well and Ronald was most complimentary and although we kept ourselves to ourselves, talking over this and that, Ronald made no mention of his daughter's departure, nor did I expect he would.

I did introduce him to Frank, the club secretary, who was as always over effusive and far too busily explaining to Ronald all the club's facilities. None the less he did say Ronald was welcome to pop in whenever he liked and if he did decide to join, he would be most welcome.

Standing there thinking about our friendship, waiting for the crematorium service to begin, I realised I had arrived far too early wanting to pay my last respects. It then occurred to me I might be the only one to see him off as he had never mentioned any other colleagues or friends, and as he went so quickly I wondered if his daughter would be able to afford to drop everything and come over from America with the grandchildren still being at school!

I continued to reflect that in the time we had been team supporters, although I had introduced him to several people I knew, I had never met any of Ronald's friends; he always seemed so self-sufficient as if he did not really need any one around.

I walked around the car park to keep my feet warm and I had to laugh to myself when I remembered his first visit to my little council flat, an accident really. Reg had asked if we could draw up the travel schedule because of the growing number of travelling supporters. "Success brings success," as Ronald liked to say.

I was no longer surprised by Ronald's ability to do things rather well, particularly when I had suggested an activity. Even, I supposed, I had pointed him in the right direction over doing things.

Anyway, I decided to take him to my flat. The first visitor, I remembered, since that stuffy council inspector came to make his yearly formal check that everything was in order in the flat.

Thinking back I suppose it must have been season three of our friendship.

Anyway I took him up to my first floor flat and he seemed a bit nervous but I thought it would be in order to have him to my place, as we had piles of lists to sort out and the local library has limitations to the spread of papers and the crabby librarian is always quick to complain.

I smiled to myself, as I remembered his amazement at meeting Jimmy, my budgerigar, and how he had laughed when Jimmy had sat on his finger and pecked at the piece of cake I had given him to hold.

A warm memory of Ronald to treasure, I thought.

Another twenty minutes, thank goodness. I glanced at my watch, the allotted time for Ronald's cremation service.

My mind drifted back to our visit to the Working Men's Club in the out of season months. He had seemed fascinated watching the snooker being played on the club's tables and this caused me to ask him one Saturday if he would like a go? He was quite enthusiastic about my idea and so we had a little practice and I must say I was very impressed how he picked up the game so quickly and I thought my tuition was spot on.

Well that season I was one of the top twenty players in the club – well just about. It was quickly clear Ronald had a lovely cue action, quite natural, and a really sharp sense of judgement on the weight of ball necessary for the pot.

Thinking about it now, I realise he actually pushed me sometimes in what became our regular games and even though he never actually beat me, there were times when I wondered if he didn't hold back a bit!

But, standing there remembering they were happy days, I taught him all sorts including poker and darts I was amazed to think he had never played before. Of course I never asked why but to be honest he wasn't much cop at darts but snooker, well another season at the table and he could have been good. As I think about it, I bet he could have made the club's top ten.

Stamping my feet and clapping my hands I realised there was now quite a group gathering at the entrance to the chapel, and it seemed to me they were rather smartly dressed, talking amongst themselves. Probably early for the next service, I thought.

I looked at Roland's full name on a label by the entry door. I knew his name from the odd letter he had carried occasionally when we met and he knew mine from my council tax return when I had complained to him about the outrageous increase one year. Well actually each year, and he had been very understanding but then of course we had kept carefully to our privacy arrangements and we never delved, or thought to investigate, each other's background. Happy, I suppose, thinking about it, to accept our arm's length friendship as a way of keeping the noisy, rather nasty demanding world, at bay so that we could get on in an orderly way.

It suddenly occurred to me that something was wrong; the well-dressed group of men and women must be coming to Ronald's cremation ceremony!

Just as I realised this, a young lady in a smart black coat with a bright scarf, detached herself from the group that had grown to, I don't know, a hundred people, and was coming straight towards me.

As soon as she got close enough I saw she had Ronald's slight smile and definitely his eyes. She held out a small neat hand "Well," she said "my dad said you would be here and early. I am Belinda, Ronald's daughter. I am so pleased to meet you."

She had a funny way of stressing the important words, like 'so'. Just like Ronald.

I held her hand for a second, feeling completely unnerved by the experience but smiling broadly back in response. "I'm, oh you know who I am," I tailed off.

"Dad told me lots about you ... when he ... wasn't well at all and he has written. Well actually he dictated a letter for you in the hospice and I typed it for him, but he said I should ask you for a favour, a big favour, for him and me. Would you escort me in his place, he said. You know what a sense of humour he had." And her eyes moistened and she brought out a small neat white handkerchief and dabbed her eyes.

"Of course I will. I will be most honoured," was all I could say, holding back my own emotions.

The entry door opened to the sound of organ music. I walked in with Belinda holding on to my arm, down the aisle to the front row, followed by at least one hundred and fifty men and women that filled the Chapel of Rest.

Later I could not recall the detail of the service. It was all a bit of a blur. I do remember the hymn, 'Praise my soul the King of Heaven' because I could remember that from my comprehensive school days. And I did register the last lines of another hymn which I thought cut through my confused thoughts. 'Speak through the earthquake, wind and fire, O still small voice of calm'. As I tried to balance my thoughts about my departed friend, Ronald.

The lady Canoness who was conducting the service talked at some length about 'contribution'. She used the word several times that Ronald had made to the business community. One or two smart suited gentlemen also made, I thought, gracious comments about his involvement in commerce.

I walked out with Belinda on my arm and she acknowledged graciously everyone who spoke to her. Naturally no one spoke to me and I felt no obligation to speak to any of these strangers, although strangely I did not feel particularly awkward.

Immediately outside the chapel a large black limousine was waiting and the driver had the rear door open. Belinda smiled up at me and fairly firmly ushered me aboard and the car swept off to somewhere I had given up bothering about.

Belinda squeezed my hand. "Dad was quite right, he said you being there would get me through."

She opened her handbag and drew out a letter. "Dad asked me to give you this letter after the service." I opened the letter as Belinda watched me.

The letter was typed and there were several pages ... it said;

"My dear good friend, I apologise for this letter being typed but I am not in good shape to hand write and Belinda has kindly offered to help get the things down I want to say to you.

"Firstly, your help and non-questioning over the last few years kept me going and provided me with strength to continue when just before we met I was told I had terminal cancer that the specialist could do nothing about.

"The fact that you in your thoughtful way never asked questions about my life and treated me as a friend day by day, without judgement or having to know what was going on in the rest of my life, gave me the determination to keep going, and as it turned out, a couple of years longer than the specialist said would happen.

"You will now have heard I had a business career and some have suggested some success over the years, but if I tell you the burden of the wealth I built up and the pressures from individuals, advisers, charities and others was a cross I found hard to carry, and became much more difficult as the cancer took its toll, your support and friendship unquestioning and undemanding, kept me going."

"I know", he wrote "you will be thinking he's exaggerating. Well, just get this clear, you showed me a life I had never experienced. My enjoyment learning to play snooker, and you are the better player! Meeting and talking with you and other club members was the highlight of my out of season week. My enjoyment supporting our boys' football team and our pride in their success is bright in my mind as I lay here.

"Meeting Jimmy in your comfortable, safe flat was fun and a great privilege. Old friend you taught me many things and I know my friendship was valued by you, and forgive me for not asking you to visit me over the last few days in the hospice. I want you to remember me as we were, a great team.

"Now I ask for your help. I know you and Belinda will get along and I hope you will take an interest in my daughter and my grandchildren as you have so beautifully with your own, and I have to remind you that without your good counsel and advice I would never have managed my relationship so successfully with Belinda in America.

"I have put together a little trust fund with my lawyer, the details are on the separate sheet. I hope you will accept the role as beneficiary which will allow you to visit your daughter and your grandchildren every year in New Zealand and bring the family over to see you, at least once every year.

"I hope you will be able to see Belinda and my grandchildren from time to time as I would be most grateful if in my absence they could benefit from your experience and practical judgement in a world that is getting more difficult year on year.

"Lastly, there is more than enough money in the fund to replace that clapped out shower and changing room unit our boys' team have to use, and I hope you will see this project through for me on our behalf.

"It has been a privilege to call you my friend and somehow I feel, lying here, we will meet again."

Staring through the side window with the tears streaming down my cheeks and Belinda's hand firming gripping mine, it came to me. In this unexplained, unexpected meaning of my life, today has given me a glimpse of what it's really all about.